FINISHING LINE PRESS

www.finishinglinepress.com

Slipshod and Standing

by

B.L. Makiefsky

Finishing Line Press
Georgetown, Kentucky

Slipshod and Standing

This is a work of fiction. All characters, scenes and situations are either products of the author's imagination, or are used fictitiously.

Publisher: Leah Huete de Maines
Editor: Christen Kincaid
Cover Art: Erik Schereder via Pexels.com
Author Photo: Dare'l McMillian
Cover Design: Elizabeth Maines McCleavy

Order online: www.finishinglinepress.com
        also available on amazon.com
                Author inquiries and mail orders:
                    Finishing Line Press
                    PO Box 1626
                Georgetown, Kentucky 40324
                        USA

Contents

For Annie, and Erin

Everything—self-awareness, time, reason, customs, habits—tends to make us exiles from life, but at the same time everything impels us to return, to descend to the creative womb from which we were cast out.
        —Octavio Paz, *The Labyrinth of Solitude/Life and Thought in Mexico*
                Copyright 1961, Grove Press, Inc.

There is a crack, a crack in everything
That's how the light gets in.
        —Leonard Cohen, from the song *Anthem*
                Copyright 1992, Hipgnosis Song Management

Five Hundred Miles

It was a cold night in late March and the moon rose somewhere over Kansas. The wind came screaming, unrelenting and harsh, the way it is over metal, forcing me to shelter behind my pack. I stuffed a t-shirt into my knit hat and pulled it down to cover my face, peering through it like a mask. I was bound for home and classes on a freight train out of Amarillo—almost broke, exhausted, happy.

The train stopped. I moved to the front of the car—an empty automobile carrier with sides like a guard rail rising three levels—and stepped into the night. Fields still slumbered in dark winter, flat to the horizon where low stars and distant farm lights mixed. With luck, I'd ride as far as Chicago.

After a two-year absence, I had been eager to return to the university and finish my degree. But this night, in this cold place, I was having second thoughts. What did sitting behind a desk have to offer? Childhood—childish?—dreams, though numbed by the years, danced in my head. I was going to be a fireman, tennis pro, race car driver, forester, baseball player; poet. At college I floundered in one program or another, searching for answers, yet hardly knowing the questions to ask. School, I was convinced, was not going to bring out my best self, so I left to pursue what I thought a more worthy life. *What's the use of all that noise and money?* asked the Tang Dynasty poet Han-shan, named for the place he lived, Cold Mountain. His words became my calling. Freed from the weight of expectations and a career track, I wandered, trespassed, dared—and moved in awe of a new world.

On the road I felt at once both centered, and unhinged; there were no wrong turns. Not knowing in what railyard (or backyard), or under what tree or star I'd spend the night, I lived in the moment—a delightful anxiety—perhaps out of fear from looking past it. Thrilled, yet scared, seemed to be my lot in life. A joyous unease.

Of course, dropping out and leaving were easy; coming back whole, and having something to say, less so.

Now the train's brakes hissed, it shook and lurched, and I scampered back on. The swaying, windswept car made more conventional rides—bounding along in the cab of an 18-wheeler, for example, or sharing the bed of a truck in Mexico with a drove of pigs—appear first class. Wherever I kneeled—even lying down—the wind penetrated to my bones.

The train moved with all the speed of a weather front. Until it didn't. At a long and captive layover outside a small town south of Wichita—I followed the tracks on a road map—I slept much of the following day.

Woke up, plucked a freeze-dried beef with potatoes from my pack, and added boiling water from my small gas stove. This train apparently was going nowhere.

Dozing, I missed the first eastbound that rolled into the deserted yard, and waited until dark for the next.

I would not be alone on this one. Two Mexican teenagers, laughing and coatless, dashing and daring, jumped from a boxcar as the train slowed, beckoning me to follow. I didn't comprehend. "Where to?" I yelled. "Adónde?"

"La máquina! La máquina!" The younger one shouted, pointing to a second locomotive toward the front of the train, coupled to the main engine back-to-back. I followed their lead. We reached the engine, climbed its steps, and made ourselves at home on the narrow floor.

"Yo soy Mark," I told them. "Mark Silver."

"Arnulfo," said the younger boy. The older one seemed distant, yet at the same time watched me with a closeness that was unnerving. He wouldn't tell me his name. Perhaps if I had had a mirror, I wouldn't have trusted the person in it either. The two were cleaner-looking than me. Their hair was cut, their faces smooth—if indeed they were old enough to use a razor. I had a good beard going, and shoulder length hair. They were better dressed as well, however insufficiently, in shirts and trousers. I had on five layers, flannel and wool, including a down jacket and rainsuit. The Michelin Man from hell.

"Hermanos?" I asked.

"Primos," Arnulfo said. Cousins.

Spanish was at least one course I had finished at school. Arnulfo said they hoped to find work, and send money home. They had nothing to eat. I gave them a freeze-dried meal of something or other (they all taste the same after a while) which they tore into and devoured dry, like cereal. He said they'd hopped a train some days ago in El Paso, and survived the frigid nights hunkering down in deserted engine rooms, drinking the potable water there. In the warmth of this new shelter, my sleeping bag now draped over the three of us, I would survive too.

The train's rhythms were riveting, even hypnotic from our uneasy berth, at best like the rocking of a cradle. Or, at worst, the back-and-forth churning of a washing machine. And we were the oversized, unbalanced load that hadn't set off any alarms. Yet. Announcing itself at every crossroad, the train whistle (or horn) from the lead engine was unbearably loud, its frequency indicating the size of towns we rumbled through, and my heart skipped a beat—as it still does, to this day—listening to the unquiet wonder of it piercing the darkness.

Crossing the heartland, I thought of perhaps the first whistle I'd ever heard, alongside my brother a lifetime ago in an Iowa motel room near tracks, and of a train I'd been on too, a dateless journey into the night with my father somewhere near Niagara Falls. Trips I cannot put into context other than to say there was a train, night, a whistle, family. Plaintive sigh—or bold warning—the sound of a train is more or less a wrinkle in time that announces the past is ever present, and the present—in the blink of an eye—is already past. Everything is moving. Even when it isn't.

As the train eased into a small yard in central Kansas in the middle of the night, a man entered our locomotive, stumbled upon us and abruptly left. Spooked, the boys and I fled that engine at the next stop, literally hit the ground running, found an open door down the line and thrust ourselves into a dank and empty boxcar. At once, and in silence, we worked the heavy ironlike doors almost closed, leaving them open just enough to breathe in the bitter fresh air. The collective fear of being locked in, and entombed in this bleak car needed no translation.

Moving through the din and darkness of morning, staring through the narrow gap in the doors at the tree line across the tracks, I had the improbable, magical feeling that wherever we were going, wherever we ended up, I'd been to. Trains can turn your world upside down like that. For much of my life I'd gazed longingly at tracks, steel rails that seemed to beckon and bend and dissolve in the heat, disappearing in a destiny of their own beyond anything I could imagine, and the sound of a coming train—the whistle in the air, the humming of the ground—was an invitation to jump aboard; a song I had to know. Looking back at that time and the wisdom of taking such risks, today I wonder if I had lost my mind—or was simply more willing to find it.

Toward dawn we approached Kansas City, its bright lights spilling through the peephole of our boxcar doors, reminding me that I was one step—or yard—closer to home. The old desire to return, fit in, be stamped and graded pulled at me as relentlessly as the wind had pushed. I was torn between Cold Mountain, Han-shan's world, and the one chasing approval. I came to the understanding that the road away—painfully, joyfully—frames what home is and is not, as well as the people you run from, or to. The road back is merely one seeking acceptance, and I wanted to come in from the cold.

Freezing, almost delirious, wearing every last shred of clothing I had, I thought of grabbing my pack and sleeping bag—again covering the three of us—and jumping from the train.

Railroad security, however, would spare me that. Drifting in and out of sleep, I hadn't realized that we were stopped. Suddenly a flashlight in our faces. Another man barked his *what-the-fuck* at us. They forced us off the train, searched, handcuffed and sat us down, like stones on a stone wall, guarded by one agent as two others searched one-by-one the remaining cars with their imposing Maglites.

The great yard shook with life in the early morning. Tens and tens of tracks merged and straightened and curled like a sea of black snakes as cars of all shapes, tall as bulldozers and flat as dominoes, were joined or uncoupled amidst the clamor of bells. The smell of diesel was thick like mud. Switchmen sprung up like jacks-in-the-box, jumping and hollering to rearrange whole trains with a whisk of their wrists and lanterns, their sharp cries splitting the frosted blue-gray air. I thought of Studs Terkel. Sinclair Lewis. Gary Snyder. Marty Robbins.

I was certain that my life before this moment had been wasted.

Wearing tight blazers and pencil thin neckties, the two agents who busted us seemed out of place in this expansive yard teeming with workmen in coveralls. But they, too, had roles, and drove us to a half-lit modern brick building less than a mile away. Within was a congeries of other smells: coffee, vinyl, floor wax, smoke. One agent led the Mexican teens to another room and then went to search for the janitor who spoke Spanish, while the other interrogated me at his desk.

He leaned forward and asked, "Are you a Christian?"

"I suppose," I said, thinking perhaps it was a test, and that I'd won something. Like a real train ticket. "Not really," I quickly added.

"But you don't mind me asking," the agent said in a tone almost—but not quite—apologetic.

"No, I don't mind." But I did.

"Well, then, what are you?"

"Human, on both sides," I said. "Grandparents, too." I had faith in that.

He sighed, stacked some papers, and asked if I had any drugs or a Buck knife in my gear, the latter which he clearly coveted. I had neither, and little else other than a few granola bars and some change in my pockets. He returned to his paperwork as I again thought of home—Michigan was more than 500 miles east—and my time away from it. Whatever it is that young people search for, I was on the hunt, looking for a life without adornment, blather and harm, and I was inexplicably drawn to trains. Perhaps the attraction was simple; the tracks led away from home, school and a predicable life. But tracks, of course, run in both directions, and home, as they say, is where your story begins. At times, telling mine seems within reach.

Finished with his report, the agent took a phone call, then put the receiver down. "The highway is a few miles from here," he said, nodding toward my pack. "Maybe you'll find a ride." And I thought, it's a weary thing, the simple act of holding your thumb out and relying on the charity of others. I wasn't looking forward to it. I thought, too, of the teens, soon to be homeward bound themselves with the clothes on their backs and probably not much more. Just then I turned to the waiting room to see them enter, and sit. The older, quiet one raised his still-cuffed hands and smiled at me through the glass.

"Pablo," he said, loud enough for me to hear. "Pablo from Magdalena de Kino. Vaya con dios, Marcos."

"They'll be detained for Immigration," the agent said, following my gaze. "You're free to go. But I'm warning you: We have what we need to know about you. Do not ride the Santa Fe through Kansas again."

And I wouldn't. Not through Kansas.

Feldman's Curve

It was the summer Marilyn Monroe was found dead, and Spider-Man born. It was the year of the Cuban Missile Crisis, too, though world events were not on the Cubs minds; only baseball mattered. The boys lived the game morning, noon and night and what these 11 and 12-year-olds lacked in skills they found in dreams, where wooden bats crackled like Zorro's whip as they smacked balls over fences, and their leather gloves— which they slept with—snagged them from thin air and lofty heights, highlight reel catches that brought frenzied crowds to their feet. In dreams they were undefeated, took the pennant, and returned to school in the fall as tough *hombres*.

But here they were: Down a run in the last inning of their last game, and they hadn't won a thing. Cellar-dwellers. The Cubs knew well the *mercy rule*, and mercy was just.

Through loss after heart-breaking loss, failure after failure— brooding, magnificent, end-of-the-world failure—failure looking back at them each morning in their reflections at the bottom of empty cereal bowls as they reached for their *Breakfast of Champions*, failure that hit them like a truckload of hurt each time they unloaded their equipment at practice, their bats and gloves seemingly full of holes, failure that beat snot and swagger from them (a swagger they'd go on searching for much of their adolescence) clinging to them like their sodden jerseys did that hot and joyless summer, *lives in ruin* failure—losses they couldn't shake off, like a tic that had burrowed under the skin of their wan and fragile selves to infect the whole of their secret lives, and no matter how angrily they might kick in frustration an empty can down the street on their walk home after yet another defeat, or throw stones at a stray cat—with the same success they had hitting the cutoff man earlier—they failed to vanquish it, failure. And once home, in a final act of rage and resignation, they'd sling their wet jerseys onto their bedroom floors all the while telling mothers and fathers or sisters and brothers everything was *just fine.*

Through all the doom and gloom, the team knew why they lost: It was their coach's fault, the unflappable Mr. Feldman. Who never said an unkind word to anybody. Not to the opposition, and never to umpires. When a call didn't go the Cubs way, he'd say, Guys, we'll get the next one. Or tomorrow is a new day. Or keep trying.

Such calm didn't sit well with third baseman Mark Silver. He couldn't hit a lick but swung freely at the coach, low blows all; Vincent Feldman was an easy target. Apart from his smile, nothing on his face fit or endeared you to look his way. His chin was closer to his right ear than you'd think possible, and his nose just hung there like a windsock on a windless day. A train wreck of a face that made everything he did—Silver was certain—not just lopsided, but wrong, too.

Feldman wasn't about winning at all costs. He wasn't about winning at any cost. "We can't even win ugly," Silver would complain to his teammates.

Across the diamond this last game of the season—the other side of the standings, as well—were the undefeated Dodgers, whose coach's name no one would remember. He was built like a fireplug, but the plug loose. He badgered umpires, and ridiculed his own team when they didn't play well. And many on the Cubs wanted to play for him. Or so they said. He was a winner, Feldman a loser. He coached the all-stars. Vincent Feldman didn't coach all-star games.

"Nice guys finish last!" taunted the Dodgers from their dugout that day. "Second place is the first loser!" they shouted. Second place? A dream to the Cubs. They were still looking for their first win. *Everyone plays*, was Feldman's mantra. There's no I in T-E-A-M, he'd preach. It's *Us*. The boys came out swinging, as best as they could.

Roddy Braun was pitching for the Dodgers, he with a cannon for an arm and a quiver of two arrows, ungodly fast and dipsy doodle slow. Both lights out. He was also Silver's best friend, and their mothers were sitting together in the stands at Palmer Park in Northwest Detroit this warm August evening. As providence would have it—providence being as much a part of the game as the stitches on the ball—Silver came to bat in the last inning with the tying run on third base, and two outs.

Roddy stared down his catcher, took a deep breath, glanced at Silver with murder in his heart, and reached back. Strike one. Hard down the middle. The bat never left Silver's shoulder. He glanced at the catcher's mitt to see if the ball was truly there. *Should have known what was coming*, he said to himself. *You never even saw it*, said another voice—also his. He thought about stepping out of the batter's box, stretching, swinging his bat free and easy. But didn't. Vik, the Cubs runner on third, was dancing down the line, daring to go home at the crack of the bat, or wild pitch. Silver raised his bat above his head and gripped it tight, too tight. Roddy threw something outside and off-speed that he lunged at. Strike two.

Now Silver tapped the plate with his bat. Another strike, and the long season would be over. The thought of making the last out weighed heavily on his thin shoulders. He wanted to be a hero, drive in the tying run and do right by his team. His chest heaved, and his restless heart pounded against the rough inside of his jersey where the word *CUBS* was stitched. Roddy would not quick-pitch him, and gave Silver a moment to collect himself. Mark glanced at the stands, and wondered what their mothers might be talking about. If they even kept score. He saw Vik standing on third, looking at the ground, his shoulders slumped. Their third base coach was shaking his head. Maybe he could get a piece of the ball, put it in play, he thought. Maybe the infielder would boot it and he'd be on first, the game tied. Again Silver wanted to step out of the batter's box, but lacked the confidence to actually do it, and delay the game. Time seemed as unstoppable as Roddy's fastball.

Scowling, arms folded, the red-faced Dodger coach yelled in to home plate, "Finish up now, son." As if Mark Silver was late making some kind of purchase, the lights dimmed and the store closing. The situation was larger than he had an answer for, and he felt very small.

The Dodger bench was on its feet, screaming for the final strike. It was funeral quiet on the Cubs side. But just as Roddy went into his windup, Feldman asked for a timeout. The Cubs collective jaws dropped. He'd never done that. Some of them were jumping up and down, as if they'd finally won something. The Dodger players hushed.

Feldman ambled over to Silver, put a hand on his shoulder. "*Stop thinking,*" he said. "React." Silver rested the barrel of his bat on the ground, and watched a few pigeons take flight from the roof of the third base dugout. He said that he couldn't hit Roddy. Felt stupid trying.

"We're all stupid," Feldman said. "You, me, the umpire, and especially that coach over there." He motioned to the other team without looking. "You've got two strikes against you. But what counts here is how we hold our heads. Not our bats." He squeezed Silver's shoulder. "Just do your best. Hang tough." Mr. Feldman headed back to the dugout.

Hang tough, Silver thought, digging his rubber cleats into the batter's box. *How do you hang tough against a pitch that seems capable of splitting you in two? Coach might as well have said hang ten.*

Again, Roddy started his windup. The whole world knew what was coming. Silver choked up on the bat—and then, it happened. His raging heart quieted, as if the simple act of loosening his grip had loosened his mind. His thoughts stopped racing, and the game slowed down.

Now the pitcher seemed as big as a billboard to him, and Silver knew what he was selling. He watched Roddy bring his hands to his chest, his leg lift and stride toward him with his arm cocked. He saw Roddy's hand come forward, then the inevitable release of what looked like a puff of smoke. Less than a heartbeat later Silver made contact with the ball. Not a resounding *crack*. Not a whisper, either. A shot to the left of the mound. Vik raced home, and the Cubs screamed. Sprinting to first, Silver recalled fielding balls like this one himself when the snow had melted in April, his brother hitting them all over the place and how hard it was waiting for the league to start play. He wanted to beat the throw as much as he had wanted anything in life.

The shortstop snagged the ball and threw to first, beating Silver by a step, and the Dodger players erupted. The Cubs glumly watched them put Roddy on their shoulders, and parade around the diamond as if they were marching into history, that brash high-step cockiness of youth who are certain their path forward would remain notable, and undefeated. That one pitch, or swing or game had changed their world.

Mark Silver would remember the swing he put on the ball, a good swing, and the out he made.

Mr. Feldman brought Silver his glove, though his teammates would not look at him. Feldman smiled, his ears seeming a mile apart, that lopsided ear-to-ear smile, and in Feldman's curve, a face so without guile and menace, Silver saw that life wasn't always a straight line. The coach said that he hoped Silver would play for him again next year.

Stealing Home

My father Chollie loved to sing. In his youth he wanted to be a cantor, but ended up helping support his large family by assembling wagons at a hardware store on Michigan Avenue instead. He'd get a nickel each. That's what my grandmother told me, anyway. Not his mother, but his mother-in-law, who one day loaned him and my uncle Hal the money to start a business. They named it "Silverstein Brothers Hardware" and put up a fancy sign, but the yellow brick building on the corner across the street from Our Lady of Mt. Carmel Church in downriver Wyandotte, was—by customers and neighbors—simply called *the Jews*.

Silver is the family name now, changed from Silverstein long before the brothers hung that sign. According to my father, his teachers at Eastern High School found the pronunciation, and spelling, of *Silver* easier. Perhaps, like many immigrants then, his Russian-born parents saw the change as progress, part of becoming American. My father was always proud of the original family surname.

His first name was Charles, but my father's cousin, the singer Sophie Tucker, who'd occasionally perform across the river in Windsor, Ontario, called him *Chollie*, and that name stuck, too. When the telephone operator called our home to say there was "a person-to-person call from New York for Chollie Silver," the family knew at once who was on the line and we'd circle my father as he held the receiver up for us to hear, a twinkle in his eyes. "Chollie, come see me at the Elmwood Casino next week," Sophie would say in her thick Yiddish accent. "Bring your lovely wife and children, Chollie. There'll be a table for you."

What made Chollie sing? Whatever talent his cousin had didn't rub off on him. Her voice was, like herself, large and theatrical; and his, needle thin. His simple tunes from a bygone era, like *Boogie Woogie Bugle Boy* or *Daisy Bell*, amused me as a child, but over the years the singing would diminish his authority in my eyes. I didn't want a father—though almost six feet tall, with biceps like iron—who responded to adversity with song. I wanted one who packed a gun, fought fires or played baseball for a living like the Tigers second baseman Frank Bolling, who lived down the street from the store.

Painter, plumber, electrician, entrepreneur—Chollie was all these things. But I judged him by who he wasn't: Wyatt Earp. Elvis Presley. Babe Ruth. I wanted my father to hit every question I pitched about life over the fence, but he said little. Nevertheless, he always encouraged me to sing. At the same time, my mother, a schoolteacher in Detroit, constantly urged my brother Jay, sister Debbie and me to smile.

Even today I often suppress the urge to smile because I fear what it might lead to: singing, and becoming my father. Still, there is an irrepressible chorus in my heart, a chest-thumping exultation that lays claim to this simple man. Another beat cries out as well, a lament from chasing the unattainable, his approval. Baseball, a game he also loved, was my release. Running after the ball as it arced across the sky beneath a burning sun in that endless landscape of sandlots. A spit of land, or a base, all your own to defend. The game is straightforward, and complete. *See the ball. Hit the ball. Catch the ball.* Home was where you started and ended and everything in between fit as naturally as a sunrise and sunset.

***

At the age of ten I was hired by my father to set up displays on the sidewalk, and lower the awning; sweep the floor; empty trash and break down cardboard boxes to burn in the alley; smash the broken glass of windows to be repaired on the basement workbench, and fill wooden barrels with the shards; stock and dust; and carry or wheel on a handcart the customers' purchases to their cars. In the ensuing years I fixed windows and screens, cut and threaded pipe, assembled wagons, bicycles and wheelbarrows, and made deliveries. But what I did best was hide. In the warehouse. The basement. The loft. Ducking here and vanishing, there, like a combatant behind enemy lines. No one much cared, or noticed. Except Hal.

Short, long-faced with dark bags under his eyes and marsupial-like jowls large enough to fit the sadness of the world, Hal was the youngest of my father's seven siblings, smaller even than his buxom sisters. He never stood still as if, due to his somewhat mournful appearance, he'd become a moving target. His approach, everything in its proper place—for example, insisting that we check out to the penny—helped him manage his anxiety and the crisis with his daughter, who battled addictions and mental illness. He tried hard to make the imperfect perfect, make the unkind less so, and his intensity, persistence and directness often drove customers away. Some would return later the same day and ask for my father to wait on them. Unlike Hal, Chollie could take a punch.

Eddie was a part-timer at the store who worked full time at the chemical plant. He had eight kids, was a pious Catholic and infuriated Hal with his thirty-minute bathroom breaks. I once found his collection of nudist magazines, hidden on a bathroom shelf, and took a stack of them home in a paper bag, playing *peekaboob* on the ride home to Detroit with my father. I shared the collection with friends until one day that summer after the game we burned the whole lot, each magazine, behind home plate, which made me feel sad, yet grown up, too.

Gary was younger than me, and worked at the store after school and Saturdays. There were other full and part-time workers who came and went, and by the early 1960s wages from the store helped support a handful of families. That was before a K-Mart would open nearby and siphon off much of the business; before the Lowes and Home Depots and Walmarts killed off the K-Marts and Sears.

Customers were mostly from the working-class neighborhood of small ranch houses on immaculately maintained lots: Bill Studebaker, who pushed around his wife and then spent a lot of money on her at Christmas. Frankie Brazka, the drunkest of town drunks, whose wife pinned his shopping list to his shirt. The mean-spirited Mary. The impeccably dressed and well-mannered Ray Miller, a chemist, who lived uptown. These were among the regulars, and most worked at either Wyandotte Chemical, for the city or at the nearby Trenton and Gibraltar facilities of McLouth Steel. In the rental flat above the store lived tenants, Fred, with a beer belly and congenial face, and his wife Peanuts, a wisp of a woman about five feet tall, 80 pounds, with long dark hair.

The hardware store stood in the shadow of the steeple, and wherever my deliveries would take me I only had to look for the cross in the sky to find my way back. I learned the tools of the trade there, and over the years, struggled to see the customers not as the vicious Jew-baiting thugs my grandmother had labeled them, but as dreamers of terrible dreams, immigrants as frightened of the new world as my father would soon be of mine. Thrust from one world, off-step in another, they were a disbelieving lot (despite their church-going), so drunk on their rancor for life and its narrow prospects that its simplest aberrations, a Jew on the block, for example, and later, my long hair, set them amok. In the face of such abuse, my father chose to sing, while I sulked in the warehouse, its dankness enlivened by newly arrived leather baseball gloves, a smell sweeter than spring flowers, and the rattle of the smooth-grained Louisville Sluggers still in their boxes. I'd shake them to feel less alone. I would try them all in my secret warehouse games, and knowing that I was the first to wear each mitt, and swing every bat made me the best that ever played.

***

Silverstein Brothers Hardware. Sawdust on a wooden floor. An old brass scale to weigh nails, grass seed, lead and oakum for joining iron soil pipe. Wall-to-wall shelves of solvents, soaps, oils, cleaners, greases and degreasers, goop, weed killers, adhesives and waxes. Tape and caulk. Insect repellants. Clothespins and clotheslines. Here a rare patch of bare floor fortified on three sides by waist-high 50-pound bags of play sand, Milorganite and ready-mix cement. There a wall of hammers, screwdrivers, drill bits, scrapers and chisels. Merchandise hung or stacked to the rafters:

Iron skillets, crocks, galvanized tubs, washboards, porcelain roasters, rods and reels. Alarm clocks and radios. Cookers, appliances, training wheels. Baseball gloves on a pegboard. And down one narrow aisle, all the screws, nuts and bolts that kept everything together. Everything in the physical world, that is; there was no hardware to separate the jarring parts of life, no glue for the unglued.

Past the door to the basement and a few steps up from the main floor, was the toy room. My brother and I often stole the gumballs, or sat on the shiny new bicycles. I remember dolls that I wanted to play with, but didn't. Doll houses and electric trains that I did. Beyond the set of tracks where toy engines roared, there was an opening to a back room stocked floor to ceiling with paints and stains. "An undertaker's before you bought the building. Laid out the bodies right where you keep the paint," the old-timers said. "Your prices will bury us too, Jew," they said. Proud men, my father explained when they ranted Jew-this and nigger-that. *The Customer Is Boss*, a sign over the cash register read.

Above the main floor and the one checkout counter was the "Employees Only" loft. Access to it was a staircase across from the office, its rails and overhang draped, like overgrown jungle flora, with coiled "snakes" and augers for plugged drains, fan belts of every length and diameter, trouble lights and extension cords. The steps to the loft were lined as well by fire extinguishers in bronze canisters filled with mysterious powder, and cartons waiting to be carried up, or down. Haphazard rows of housewares in squat boxes and window shades in slim ones (along with a Star cutting machine) dotted the loft floor. The view was of the entire main floor below, including the rack of shotguns and hunting rifles alongside the cash register, and next to it, a glass showcase of Timex and Westinghouse watches, fishing lures, compasses and hunting knives.

The loft had a musty library-like smell, and although the lighting was poor, the boxes crowding it were perfect shields to hide behind, and read. Better yet, I'd turn a square of open floor into a diamond where I'd spread my collection of baseball cards, organizing teams of all left-handed batters (like myself) against all righties. I made Al Kaline and Nellie Fox the captains, and quietly called the play-by-play. Minnie Miñoso batted. Willie Mays and Ted Williams, too. Until Hal intervened. I then reluctantly pocketed the cards, a pit in my stomach for leaving the game that was the air I breathed for a world that was dragging me along, and one that I was expected to enter.

The office shelves overflowed with parts, special orders and returns, and Chollie's singing filled every void that merchandise didn't. In one corner a sink, towel bar and mirror. (The warehouse served as our refrigerator.) In another, a large wooden desk, and above it, a pinup of Marilyn Monroe, nude from the waist up, hung on the wall along with the Rigid Tool Company's monthly calendar of models in swimsuits leaning over the industry's machinery. Catalogs and a large binder from the wholesaler covered the desk. Sanders, rug cleaners and other machines for rent stood upright on the floor. Past these, a door led to a dank passage, the wide barn-like doors of the warehouse, the rickety stairs to the rental flat and, at the end of the hall, a door that opened on a quiet street, Superior Boulevard.

There were several dark or poorly lit rooms in the basement, where loose mortar on cinderblock walls seemed to crumble from the weight of the ages. In one cavernous and unheated recess, newly assembled bicycles and wagons were stored. Over winter, it included lawn mowers, Schwinns, Huffys and Red Flyers that hadn't sold. Layaways, too. Those with pickup dates, and others abandoned by the customer but not yet returned to stock. Each of them with a story of its own. Toward the rear of the basement was a battered wooden elevator the size of a walk-in cooler that even my brother was too frightened to explore. He said there were caskets and bones there, and a blood pit below the floor; an unsettling thought, especially if I was alone using the one bathroom nearby, or repairing a window. Above the elevator, the shaft disappeared into a dark and unfathomable space.

The basement was quiet except for the faint tunes on the radio that drifted down the stairs. On Saturday afternoons my father let me put the game on, the volume turned up to hear the mellifluous voices of Tiger broadcasters Ernie Harwell and George Kell, their southern drawl music to our ears. Away from the sound of the radio and string of overhead bulbs, the basement was like a dungeon. If someone turned off the lights—there was one switch at the top of the stairs—either by accident (my father) or on purpose (my brother), fear seeped into my bones from the ground up.

The one phone in the store was a payphone attached to the wall near the main entrance. Encased in hardcover, the Detroit phonebook dangled from a short chain above the radiator. For a dime, anyone—neighbors, customers, employees—made calls and shared their lives with the world. It was there where I overheard more than I wanted, and understood even less. Hal's anguished calls from his wife, my aunt, or conversations with the psychiatrist concerning his daughter. Hal calling the Wayne County Department of Social Services to report that the tenants upstairs were behind on their rent. My mother calling to see how late my father and I would be for dinner. It was there where Hal listened patiently to customers who couldn't pick up their layaway because they'd lost their job. Or spouse.

There where my father placed orders from the "want-list," which he kept on a spiral notepad, his precise letters like an army of black ants filling the page margin to margin. How I would have loved to fill my needs with a simple call, should I have been able to come out of hiding and speak up.

"*Dad, is that you? I need a hug.*"

"*Dad, why is the customer boss?*"

"*Dad, why doesn't Mrs. Studebaker come in anymore?*"

***

Bill Studebaker. No one touched him. Hal said he'd been a sailor, tossed overboard by the Navy. "No one pushes me around!" Studebaker yelled once at my father about a charge. Chollie simply said okay, and adjusted the bill.

It's Saturday, early afternoon. I see Studebaker on the floor below. He's a handsome, mercurial fireman with graying temples. I'm turning sixteen, almost too tall to remain hidden behind boxes in the loft. Thunder beats down on the stamped tin ceiling overhead. Fred and Peanuts in the apartment upstairs, at it again. Their punch-drunk world of abuse, welfare benefits, alcohol and dog shit. Studebaker grips a new hammer, puts it back. Even his tattoos have muscles. Customers seem to know things—about drinking, partying, violence—I want to know, but I fear knowing *them*. They appall and attract me and I don't know what to do with these wildly dissimilar emotions. The loft is a safe distance. I watch others milling in the aisles below, lost in thoughts of what needs attention and what can wait; gifts to the homes they wreck and the women they hurt. Sometimes customers stop dead in their tracks and I see up close their red-rimmed eyes, hear their heavy breathing and maybe a word or two they utter to themselves. I sense they want something more in their lives, some addition, or maybe one less thing in need of repair. I sense, even at that age, we're all a little unsure and lost.

But not when I look at cool Bill Studebaker. Nothing about him suggests weakness, or need. Now he's holding court with my father and a few other men by the basement stairs, and over the radio's pregame chatter, I hear the words *attempted rape*. A short time later, I ask my father about it. He's uneasy.

"An incident near Superior and Biddle last night," he says. "Bill was the first to respond."

"To what?"

"They say a man can't, can't, you know, get it up, if he's drunk," he stammers, his face beet red.

"They say? You mean you don't know?"

He says nothing, and retreats to his office. I hear him singing.

"Strike up the band," I shout after him, turn and see Bill Studebaker smirking.

I knew little about alcohol, a bit more about sex, but nothing of the two combined and I was furious that my father knew so little as well. Such knowledge, I was convinced, was passage into manhood and that Chollie was ignorant of it dashed any hopes I had of crossing effortlessly there, fully armed. I flipped on the light to the basement and stomped down the stairs, went to the workbench, took a glob of putty from the can and tossed it with all my might against the wall.

Splat! "Fuck!" I screamed.

Grabbed and tossed another one.

Splat! "Fuck!"

Splat! "Fuck!"

You don't know shit, I thought. *Splat!*

***

One Saturday Chollie asked me to spy on Bill Studebaker from the loft. I was thrilled he gave me this task, *store detective*, as most of my assignments came from my uncle. Chollie must have known, too, that when business was slow I often perched there, reading. Day dreaming.

A week earlier a Timex watch had disappeared from the showcase. Hal then removed the key, kept on a hook near the cash register, and said he thought it was Bill. "I left him alone on the floor," said Hal. "I went downstairs to use the bathroom."

"Absurd," said my father. "He's a good customer. The best." He wanted to prove Hal wrong.

Studebaker was a painting contractor as well as a fireman, and seemed at ease whether in paint-stained bibs, or uniform. He rescued cats from trees and drunks from alleys and told *True Detective*-like stories. My father looked up to him. Once Studebaker started to walk out of the store with a new paintbrush that he hadn't paid for. "Could happen to anyone," I remember my father saying.

I didn't catch Studebaker stealing that day, but weeks later Hal did, and threatened to press charges. Studebaker said he was an alcoholic, and he started to cry. Hal ushered him to the office to see Chollie. I was sitting on the steps to the loft, across from them. Chollie said that calling the police could end Bill's career at the fire department, and ruin him. He told Bill not to steal from them again, that he was too good a customer for Silverstein's to lose. He put his arm around Studebaker, who rested his head on my dad's shoulder, an intimacy I longed for. Chollie would splash Old Spice on his face mornings before leaving the house, a scent my sister and I thought of as ours, inseparable from the man, and I wondered if the thief drank that in, too.

Years later, when I was a sophomore in college, I would recall the tolerance shown Bill Studebaker when Chollie busted me for a packet of marijuana he had found when I came home on break. He walked into the store—I was already there—and said he wanted a word with me. I sat down near the main entrance on bags of fertilizer warmed by the sun. Beads of sweat gathered on his forehead. He didn't put his arm around me. *What should I do?* Chollie asked. I'd rather he smacked me right there, if that was helpful, rather than see his anguish. He'd known exactly what to do with Studebaker; why not with me? I didn't ask what he was doing in my closet, thanked him for not calling the police, and went to the basement.

Splat. Splat. Splat.

***

The Silverstein brothers rewarded "regulars" with a 10% or 20% discount, depending on the item's wholesale cost which was marked by letters in black crayon according to a secret code created by Hal, *hilfunsgot*. Each letter in the word corresponded to a number, one through nine, and the t stood for zero. For example, a plastic drop cloth with a price tag of $2.49 would have the letters *hnt* marked below it, indicating $1.60, its cost to us. Some of my most awkward moments occurred when a customer asked for his or her 10%. I'd then have to find Hal or Chollie to determine if so-and-so was a member of this exclusive club, and entitled to a discount.

The other day, my brother Jay told me that *Hilf Uns Got* is Yiddish for "Help Us God."

The hardware store gave solace, if not purpose, to many men; the church may have been across the street, but Silverstein's was their temple. Shuffling from aisle to aisle, some never wanted to leave. Gary, who worked for us part-time, and I had an award of our own for the most irritating of the lot: "Shmuck of the Month." It was a blue shoulder patch that simply said, in gold lettering, "Shmuck," kept alongside the cash register. We never actually handed it out, and only nodded to one another when the right customer, at the right moment, nominated himself. John Czymanski, who'd loiter until closing time, won two months in a row. Another time the reward went to an immigrant in his twenties who spoke little English but knew the word *Jew*, which he spit like a curse as he left the store empty-handed. Frankie Brazka won it after he leaned out his car door window one day to swear at us, and fell to the curb. We had just finished loading his trunk and were walking away when he started to drive off, wagging his finger and cursing at us for no apparent reason. His door opened, he fell to the pavement and yet in the blink of an eye bounced back into the driver's seat, seemingly unharmed. Pulled the car door shut and cursed us again.

Chollie would not have been pleased to learn that we treated any customer, however drunk or abusive, with disrespect. I held onto that blue patch with gold lettering for a long time, long after the store closed and my father's death.

***

A low rumbling shook the ceiling, as if a storm approached. "Fred's moving the furniture," Hal said with resignation, his jowls sagging even more than usual. *Moving the furniture* meant the couple upstairs, Fred and Peanuts, were fighting. If Hal was busy with a customer, he'd ask me to go tell them to knock it off. I'd pick my way around the empty beer cans and dog shit on the backstairs and pound on their door. Once I saw Peanuts with bruises on her face. Hal might call social services, but never evicted them.

On one trip to the upstairs flat I saw 12-year-old Tommy, over six feet tall and built like a linebacker. He lived down the street and smelled as sour as the chemical plant. Some younger boys and girls surrounded him, sitting on the steps, watching him jerk-off a puppy. I returned to the basement, opened the can of putty.

Splat! "Fuck!" I screamed. *Splat!* "Fuck!"

From putty I could shape what I willed, a perfect ball to unleash, with sound effects—in the quiet of this dim room where not even the mice squeaked—as real as the *thwack* of a major league fastball hitting the catcher's glove. I threw hard, striking out the world that wouldn't fit back into the can, and this neighborhood where the adults were fucked, the women beaten, the kids unwell and even the dogs violated.

***

Crammed with as many items as Hal could tastefully assemble, the large storefront windows, one facing each street, lit up the drab intersection. Lawn implements and garden tools in the spring, and as the months went by, baseballs and bats, tennis rackets, beach chairs and beachballs, coolers, barbecue grills, rods and reels, roasters and pumpkins, snow shovels and sleds. "Balance, not glitter," Hal said one day, as I helped him position a mannequin on a stepladder holding a paintbrush in her hand just so. A can of exterior paint, label facing out, stood near the bottom rung. "This isn't Saks Fifth Avenue. It's 10th Street. Polack Town."

I told him that I finally got ahold of one the other day. It would have been my first home run in Pony League, but I stopped at third. "I hit the ball 300 feet, into the next field. I creamed it."

"Why did you stop?"

"There was no coach at third base. Half the team screamed from the dugout for me to go home. The other half, to stay. I didn't know what to do. By the time I turned around to look, the ball was in the shortstop's glove. I was stranded on third when the inning ended."

I didn't tell Hal the worst of it. My father was in the stands.

"You could've gone home," he said after the game. "You had a home run."

***

Although Chollie was devoted to my mother, his business and faith, the road was his mistress. Ticking off the miles and songs, carefree and healthy, he'd drive us places when we were kids: Niagara Falls, Washington, D.C. (to meet our congresswoman, Martha Griffins), Grand Canyon, Las Vegas, California and Upper Michigan, where he'd swim alone in frigid Lake Superior.

On Christmas Eve we'd head downtown. For the most part my father followed the middle road in all things; our family was as distant from the occasional Christmas tree at one end of our block as we were from the Hasidim at the other. But as Chollie nosed his butter and cream-colored Packard past the gaily lit houses beyond our neighborhood, past the inner-city streets he had known so well as a mailman, his excitement was palpable as we navigated—the way Detroit streets were laid out—one spoke after another in a wheel that also had us churning in it. At its hub, downtown glittered as if it were filled curb-to-curb with broken glass, and the stars themselves appeared strung like pearls from streetlamps, trees and buildings.

"A real festival of lights," my father would boast, then sigh, as he named each skyscraper. In spite of it helping secure his livelihood, Christmas seemed forever to be a lump in his throat. He would turn the car around by the dark warehouses along the river. I'd remember the darkness behind the lights.

***

Mary didn't want me to wait on her. What was it that she bought? Nails, sandpaper, putty? The mean ones never spent much. She was a squat woman with a full head of bushy gray hair and a face like a clenched fist. Typhoid Mary, Hal called her. She saw me behind the cash register.

"Home from school?"

I nodded. The job was mine Christmas break and summers, and I labored with a mixture of enthusiasm for Friday paydays, and dread that I had to show up.

"Need the money for a haircut?"

I didn't answer.

"You look like a pussy," Mary said. "The boy's a damn pussy." She walked up and down the aisles, searching, I think, for my father. "Pussy," she shouted louder each time, trying to flush him out.

He was in his office, ignoring her rage. I heard him singing, *Daisy, Daisy. Give me your answer do. I'm half-crazy...*

"Pussy," Mary said as my uncle rang her up.

"A full mind is an empty bat, Mary," Hal said (quoting Branch Rickey, he'd tell me later). Mary stared at him. "I know a lot of jerks with short hair and clean shaves," Hal added, giving her change, and at the same time telling her, in Yiddish, to go take a dump in the ocean.

"Damn pussy," she said again over her shoulder as she left, slamming the door.

Did Chollie agree with Mary? Or was he afraid of her? I wasn't surprised to feel unwelcome in conservative Wyandotte, but since my return from college, relations between my father and I had deteriorated, too.

There was the war, always the war. Vietnam went on forever, or so it seemed, spanning high school and college, leaving college and returning, spring trainings and World Series, campaigns and elections. My father believed the government and LBJ, while I hardly trusted the authority of toothpaste. My brother Jay joined the air force. Now, twenty miles upriver from the store, Chollie's city of lights, the city he loved, was in flames: civil unrest in the country had spread like wildfire, and the 1967 Detroit riot was underway. My sister, at home, then I at work confronted Chollie over the sale of shotguns to his lily-white customers. "They only want to defend themselves," he said, reminding me that he fought for the civil rights of Blacks and Jews in the post office before I was born. "A man's home is his castle," he added, retreating to his office. We argued throughout that summer.

One morning on our way to the wholesalers, weaving in and out of the rifle-ready National Guard in their Jeeps in the war-torn inner-city streets, Chollie asked about my girlfriend Kristen. I had spent the past weekend at her rented cabin near Lake Michigan, where she was a lifeguard at the state park. He was pleased that I was not, in his words, a "fairy," but dismayed that I was seeing a *shiksa*.

"Where did you meet?" he asked.

"Around," I said.

"Have you joined any Jewish student groups at college?"

"I'm not a joiner," I said.

"Seems like you joined plenty of marches," he said.

The intersection of sex and protest. That's where we met. I didn't tell my father that. If I had opened up—if I knew how to—it'd overwhelm him. Me, too.

"Just around."

Kristen and I first eyed one another on a bus to Washington, D.C. She carried a homemade sign, "Patriots burn draft cards. Traitors burn children." We met again the next day at a bar in Georgetown. Tear gas had moved us inside. I told her about Typhoid Mary. She told me about growing up in the Thumb—her father was superintendent of schools there—as flat and dull a land that you can imagine, aside from the Lake Huron beach where she partied.

The Revolution was ours. We were going to fix things. Who could've guessed that change would come crawling? That the struggle for equal rights would outlive us? That the war would go on for eight more years? A civil war, too. Fathers against sons. The Great Society. The summer of love. Peace now.

***

My father and I rode to the store in silence for most of the last summer that we worked together. I was doing the driving by then, as his medications made him sleepy. He'd fiddle with the radio, listening to the news, then a station from Windsor that played the old songs. One morning he wanted to take the new Interstate, I-75, which had just been completed at the expense, he said, of the thriving Black commercial district it cleft in two. As the highway swept past Tiger Stadium, he talked about the games that we saw together. I remembered Norm Cash bashing one over the right field roof and how we both stood in wonder that night, tracking the flight of the ball as it sailed over the third deck and past the light towers. He then told me about the great ones he'd seen play at the corner of Michigan and Trumbull: Ty Cobb, Heinie Manush, Goose Goslin, Schoolboy Rowe. And he'd talk about Hank Greenberg. Above all—in my father's eyes—a Jew. "Wouldn't play on Yom Kippur," he beamed, then started to sing *Take Me Out to The Ball Game*. I joined in, and we shouted together a final huzzah, "...I don't care if I never get back!" We carried on about the team's current pennant fight with Boston—he said it was Greenberg's grand slam in the last inning of the last game that won it in '45—and our all-time Detroit lineup: Kaline, Kell, Kuenn, Cochrane, Cobb... Outside the old ballpark Chollie and I found refuge in the boy in us each, and I didn't want the ride to end.

A short time later I pulled up to the store and, thinking that he had dozed off, quietly exited the car to let him be. Before I closed the door my father's head jerked, and he said, "That was some homerun." I thought of the one I didn't hit. "The one that cleared the roof," he said. "Stormin' Norman Cash."

***

Chollie was tired and looking forward to retirement. He wanted a son who, if he would not study law or medicine, would step in, run the business and open a chain of hardware stores. (He, Hal and another uncle had recently purchased a store in Detroit.) I looked forward only to getting on my motorcycle. He had an angry, dope-smoking kid who didn't give a damn about his politics, business or synagogue. I was falling behind at college, too, the draft bearing down on me. Nothing had prepared him for that. Nothing had prepared me for that. My antiwar activity rankled him.

I was not my father's boy. A hole opened in my life that I was destined to measure, but never fill. I dug and dug. And am still digging.

Chollie admonished me to pay more attention to school, where I was now living with Kristen. He threatened to cut off my tuition. "Leave her," he wrote me. "Cut your hair. Go to classes." The letter, as dispassionate as if he were addressing a delinquent account, infuriated me and, in the dialogue of the times, I wrote back that "Your superficiality of values not only appalls me, but underscores the chief problems of our time. It's the dawning of a new world. Don't sleep through it."

Friends of mine were irreconcilably estranged from home, and in a bizarre rite of passage, boasted of it. I too scorned what I had: a paid education, a job when I needed it and two sober parents at home. Nevertheless, a part of me wanted to sever all ties. My parents thought otherwise, and drove to East Lansing to see me. Kristen and I lived in a rambling old fraternity house across the street from campus. No sooner had my mother set foot inside than she started bewailing (we heard her two flights up) the dirt, the cobwebs, and general squalor of the place. Upstairs in our room, the size of a large closet, my father sat bolt upright on the bed, sweating buckets, staring at the wall. After a cursory introductory glance, neither parent would look again at Kristen. At dinner out that evening, she stood at the salad bar, humiliated, unwilling to join us.

Later that semester my father made good his threat, and the money stopped. I dropped most of my classes and worked at the school library, mopping floors at night and writing papers for others during the day. Kristen waited tables off-campus, feeding me when possible. Suddenly, life seemed without bounds: I didn't need my father, or so I thought, and the draft, as it turned out, didn't need me. (My mother had made certain the draft board had documentation of my every broken bone, tear, stitch, fever and bruise.) Upon notice of their decision, Kristen and I cried, then got high and made love as night settled on the lives we privately yearned for: hers—she would tell my sister years later—to win my folks' acceptance; and mine, simply to get on my bike and leave both her and them.

Northern Michigan. Canada. Pensacola. Appalachia. New Orleans. Galveston. California. I rode in all directions, working odd jobs until I ran out of money a year later and sold my motorcycle in San Francisco for $500 to a Frenchman named Pierre. I felt unbelievably rich, and—not tethered to the bike—liberated. I bought a backpack, headed to the Sierras then hitchhiked back to Michigan and moved into a cheap flat in Wyandotte, where Hal and Chollie hired me back. But in time, life without two wheels beneath me seemed as inconsequential as the sand in my pockets. I bought another bike. Used, but it seemed to handle okay.

To feel the furious, inexorable wind, or rain like a beehive at my wrist, to soar, with a fistful of throttle, kite-like and breathless into a turn— as much at the height of control as at its delirious and wobbling edge— quieted the screaming inside. That, too, must be what made my father want to sing: not because he had an exceptional voice, but he simply had no other. He masked his fear by singing. Whistling in the dark. As I am now.

**

"Shut up!" I screamed at Chollie the morning of his stroke. He had started to sing in the kitchen, then sneezed and sneezed. And sneezed. My mother was out.

I was immobile from the neck up due to a motorcycle accident the week before, and discharged from the hospital to my mother's care. The day of the crash I'd left the hardware store early, and went into a turn too fast on a back road outside Ann Arbor, regaining consciousness in an ambulance. The last thing I remembered was laughing at myself for not bringing a change of clothes. I had a date that evening.

The doctor said I was concussed badly. A shock to my nervous system, and cervical sprain. Nothing broken, only a scratch on my left shin. The bike, totaled. The helmet that likely saved my life, busted up as well.

"Shut up!" I screamed again at my father. He wouldn't stop sneezing. He went into his bedroom to lie down.

Drugs got me by. Codeine and Valium from the doctor, hashish from a friend. Sleep was difficult and not forthcoming, yet the dreaming, what I thought were dreams, was unrelenting. My journal filled with gibberish, songs, poetry, stories.

I couldn't breathe. Couldn't rest. Thought I was alert and safe, before realizing I'd been awake for days.

My father was dying.

My mother returned, and called an ambulance. There was a calmness about her as we followed Dad in her car. The trip seemed like a minor distraction to her, intermission to some unfolding drama where she had returned to her seat to find someone in it. The situation would be resolved. Arrangements made. The show would go on.

I panicked in intensive care.

As my mother completed paperwork, I had gone ahead but could not find Chollie among the rows of beds. Each patient seemed identical, as if in such a place all men are equal. Then his voice, trolling softly, a song perhaps, pulled me in, his eyes locking onto mine for a second or two. From there they would take him to a ward where beds changed occupants like revolving doors, day and night, as men in their deliriums shouted prayers or words in Yiddish and English. He held on for three more days.

***

The last night of *Shiva* I had asked my uncle how I could be so ravaged by a death I had seen coming. *Take a good look,* I had thought each time I saw Chollie. *It could be your last.*

"A man loses his father only once," said Hal. "There's no practice." His kind voice penetrated the thick stupor of that day like a shaft of light.

My mother had been chatting with my sister in the kitchen, and now brought us two whiskies from a bottle of my father's. All other family had left, except Hal. I recalled how he and Chollie kept a bottle of Canadian Club in the office Christmas week to toast, with the "regulars," the holiday and New Year. Bill Studebaker and Frankie Brazka always showed up. Typhoid Mary, too.

"You know," said my uncle, "Chollie stuck up for you."

"I don't remember much of that."

"He had dreams for you, sure. But all those times I got on you for goofing-off? Reading? He'd tell me to let it go. That maybe you had a different calling."

The taste of those words, *a different calling*, however intoxicating and sweet, burned like the whisky. Why did he take them to his grave?

***

The product I wished Silverstein Brothers stocked would've gone on the shelf with the solvents, an oversized can applied like bug spray, and be called *Fear-not*. Fear-not the drunkenness. Wife-beating. Prejudice. The thefts, the porn, the zoophilia. Fear-not the judgement I pass here, as I will be judged alike. Fear-not, above all, that my father loved me. Chollie died thirty years ago and still I hear his queer tunes, this coarse voice that didn't alter the universe yet changed mine. The game is so much bigger than our understating of it.

I'm a father now, and my young daughter also has a different calling. She sings freely, in every room of the house, off-key. She has her grandfather's eyes, a man whom she never met. Tonight she has fallen asleep on the floor of my study, where some of her toys are scattered. Dolls, and a doll house. A small wooden train set that I play with when she isn't there. She has left radio her radio on, to a distant station from across Lake Michigan in Wisconsin. The old songs fade in and out, and in that lick of space between tracks, the silence, too, crowds me unbearably.

Bear County

Bear County calls itself the "Asparagus Capital of the World," but it is no more that than Lansing is the capital of the United States. A handful of countries, as well as counties in California and Washington, grow more of the crop. But self-anointed or not, asparagus is indeed king in this northwestern Michigan county, where dozens of family-owned farms, migrant labor, sandy soil and temperate weather provided by Lake Michigan make possible the vegetable's abundance. The crop, along with the workers returning to harvest it, is the harbinger of spring and the growing season.

The county is home to the National Asparagus Festival, with a midway, 5K *Spear-it* race, parade, marching bands, farm tours, and asparagus bake-off. Events culminate with the crowning of the new "Mrs. Asparagus," who was—at the time when recent college graduate Mark Silver reported on the festivities for the weekly *Bear County Almanac* —a respected housewife representing the county's conservative values. Today festival organizers nominate instead a younger and often unwed queen because, according to the festival chairperson, "they ran out of farmer's wives."

Strawberries follow asparagus, then peaches, cherries, squash, cucumbers (pickles), apples, and at season's end, the Christmas tree harvest. The migrant population, mostly from South Texas, have a hand in each.

But there were problems. The doors to Human Services, locked for decades to all but residents, were at last flung open up and down the Lake Michigan fruit belt, and the migrants, once denied access to the system, were now often sustained by it. Farmworkers had become both casualties in the battle for equal rights, and in the government's response to it.

The balance of labor and the ingredients that went into a productive harvest fascinated the reporter. The livelihood of farm families (and, in turn, the region's prosperity) depended on "getting them apples off the trees," the Department of Agriculture's extension office director in Stillwater, the county seat, told Silver when he first moved to this rural community. He used the migrant crew leader Carlos Dávila, and farmers such as Miles VanSlyke and Jerry Brandon as other sources for his articles in the *Almanac*. Merritt Reef, his running companion who worked at the cannery, and the farmworker Sarita Madrigal also provided invaluable material. Obtaining useful information from the Department of Human Services was difficult due to client confidentiality, and its director, Nelson Roy, discouraged staff from talking to Silver. Rebekah Stern, a supervisor there, suggested that he interview Sarita and her son Jesse. The two also lived with Silver one winter before mother and son returned to Texas at the end of the pickle harvest the following year, where Sarita had earned a scholarship to Texas A&M University.

Dávila explained to Silver that the Feds, like a modern-day shaman selling snake oil, had a program for your every need. What could he offer his people? Guaranteed wages and steady employment? Health benefits and a 401(k)? He knew, too, that without the food stamps or cash assistance that his crew depended on, he might have to look the other way and hire undocumented workers each spring to go north to harvest the fruits and vegetables at VanSlyke's Lakeshore Acres, where he was foreman. And that could put VanSlyke in the crosshairs of both Immigration and the Department of Labor. A shortage of workers also meant that farmers—their own families already down in the dirt and straining to fulfill contracts—likely would have to hire additional high school students, or other locals who might want seasonal work. Some were skilled; most, not.

Silver had been at the newspaper less than a year when on a brisk spring morning he interviewed Raymond Kish, who grew several hundred acres of asparagus along with other crops outside the Lake Michigan town of Sears Harbor. The two men stood on the farmer's porch, and Silver asked how many of Kish's laborers might be, over the course of the season, undocumented. He reassured the farmer that if the information provided was incriminating, he'd not use his name, or the name of the farm.

Kish was an imposing man, over six feet tall and close to 300 pounds. He reached into his bib pocket for a plug of chewing tobacco from a small tin, and the floorboards creaked. He asked Silver to note his partially occupied migrant housing, a half-dozen squat cinderblock buildings across the road, and then pointed to over their low-slung roofs at fields of asparagus that stretched to the horizon. The sun was coming up over the house behind the farmer and Silver, and the cloudless sky was a deep blue, washed clean by the breeze off the lake. For a half-minute they stood and listened to the motorized hum of the asparagus rider and crew in the distance, the rising dust cloud marking its place. Mark also saw rows of crowns, golden in the bright morning, gone to seed, the field only partially picked.

"I need help now," Kish said, stuffing his jowl with tobacco. "Good, hard-working Mexicans, and I don't give a shit which side of the river they're born. Quote me. I don't care. I'm not gonna hire coloreds or white trash." Hoping a sufficient number of skilled migrants would return north in time for the asparagus, Kish had rolled the dice—and lost.

"Respect has its price," Dávila sighed when Silver relayed the story.

Ruggedly handsome, with a thick mustache and wave of grey-black hair, cowboy boots, jeans and crisp western shirt, Dávila looked like he could be on loan from a Hollywood movie set, where he'd be cast—with his abundant yet measured contempt for all systems that did not align with his efforts to overthrow them—as villain, or hero. *Emiliano Zapata*, thought Silver. They were talking outside the crew leader's trailer at the edge of an apple orchard. The sweet-smelling blossoms, late that year due to the cold spring, were overwhelming, and Silver felt intoxicated.

Finding the right workers was difficult, Dávila said. Some from previous harvests had moved on to better opportunities. Or the work just plain wore them down. Dávila said that, for the most part, his crew had been intact for years. They shared a past where you left school early, came back late, dropped out young, and "*la migra*," Immigration, followed you from the southern border to the Great Lakes. You swallowed so much pride along the way it eventually rotted your gut. What the alcohol had left of it. Carlos Dávila didn't blame the workers for spitting on the system, and grabbing what they could.

"Kish understands," Dávila said. "Mexicans travel as a family and have mouths to feed. The Black crews that bussed up from Florida were usually single men. And the southern whites were the hardest drinking of them all. Unreliable. Will you print what he said?"

"I can't," said Silver. He knew that what people said on Main Street, or in the fields, was different than what they wanted to read in the paper. Still, he told Dávila that he yearned to report the truth. What he saw. And who he was, and was to become, in other stories.

"The truth?" Dávila laughed. "Like fish in the sea. Each one swallowing the next and the next, until what you thought was true is unrecognizable. What you once stood for, compromised. Go overboard with it, and they'll toss you in jail."

That was too cheerless for Mark. But he'd remember their conversation years later when the director of Human Services accused Dávila and his girlfriend, the social worker Rebekah Stern, of hacking into the state welfare system to benefit his crew.

In the quiet of Bear County's scarcely populated hills and valleys, where he'd run and ski and rant unbridled in any direction, or roaming the country on lay-off from the paper, Mark Silver learned—as he had in his father's hardware store—that his unquiet emotions didn't bring the truth any closer. He came to know failure, and rejection—writing, working, loving—but faith, too, that he would find in the churn a safe path to whatever dignity his own faults allowed.

The *Almanac* was part of a group of newspapers (when printed material mattered) that covered the north, but there wasn't much to report on after the Christmas tree harvest. Winter was slow, and the snow deep.

The Right Touch

(in memory of Daisy Kornylak)

You were trying to quit. I just got started. I reached into your front pocket where you kept the loose cigarettes we had bought at Woodward's. You wore a flannel shirt and no bra. The same flannel shirt you usually wore. The same no-bra. What if you had told me not to touch you? That you weren't ready? But you didn't. Not then. Not before. They sold a lot of things at that general store. Milk, chicken feed, cowboy boots, saddles. We walked past the lit and deserted fairgrounds, the empty stables, up the hill that overlooks town and shared the first cigarette on an outcropping where we sat. Took off our shoes, dangled our feet over the edge of the cliff. Kicking, barefoot, into the unknown. Your thin calves like strands of rope. All of town sparkled in the valley below us. All the stars of the desert night above. A man could make a lot of wishes on those stars.

I wished I hadn't laughed when you said to call you *Fay Windsong*, a name that spoke to the sorrows you endured and life you now celebrated. I wished you hadn't trusted me. I wished your ex wasn't crazy, and your young son didn't have to share the one bed with you in your small cabin attached to the woodshop. I wished your father hadn't abused you. I wished my mother would like you. I wished I didn't look at you with two faces, smiling and terrified. I wished I wasn't lost, and the gravity of memory pressing down upon us with their pinholes of light showed me a path. I wished the Midwest didn't pull me back to the center, and that when I found myself in your arms, they were enough. I wished a star would fall, a sign. I wished that however long I waited on this star—a moment or millennium—its burning light held meaning. I wished your old Volvo would last. I wished I wouldn't have said, each time I left you, I loved you. And I wished I had loved you, without first having to leave. I wished I had the courage to say nothing. I wished you had said no. I wished that each star didn't beg with all its glamor to be a door to somewhere else. I wished there were more stars, and wishes came true. A bad habit, you said, when I had asked you for a cigarette that night when the ex pulled into the driveway with your boy, our ankles pinned in the twist of your blankets, the sound of his tires on the loose gravel stirring us awake.

I wished I could have stopped crying this morning. I wished I understood what part of me you reached, this wellhead you tripped. You and Daisy had returned from a workshop in L.A. on trigger point therapy. The two of you asked me if you might put into practice new techniques you learned. "No pressure, Mark," Daisy said, and we laughed. I thought I was in safe hands. She, a chiropractor, and you, a massage therapist. I was on your table, face down, nude from the waist up. I felt your hands, mostly. I wish I knew what happened. My spine tingled, my heart ripped, my soul laid bare. Afterward you comforted me, held me, and said that muscles have memory. That our bodies are shaped by pressures, more than we can know, we're made slipshod yet standing, carved up like the earth when the glaciers retreated. That we're all tear stained, on the rebound, bending toward the light.

Tonight I wish it were so.

Come Back, Sheila

Sheila. I'm drinking your coffee at your kitchen table and telling you what I think of your boyfriend who left me standing in your driveway this morning: not much. My pickup was buried under a foot of snow, so I hiked downhill to your cabin where you and Kyle had open road. You had warned me that above 6,000 feet the snow would come. Only days ago I rode my 10-speed helter-skelter down the canyon into Green Valley for supplies. No slipping and sliding then, though the ride back up was steeper than I was ready for. More on that in a bit.

I was brushing the snow off my pantlegs and didn't see Kyle by your car, when he announced, "Mark, we're going for a ride." I could use a few things, too, new gloves, maybe beer. Coffee. So I thanked him, and said, good timing. "How so?" Kyle asked, and before I could state what I thought was obvious, he added that "*me* and Sheila are going to look at property near Sonoita." You came out of your cabin about then, and waved to me. More hello, than goodbye.

The two of you got into the car. And still, although there was no traffic coming down the mountain, I thought he was turning the car around for me to get in, not backing up onto the road. A small courtesy. Kyle shows me that, now and then. When he reached behind you, behind your seat, I thought he was opening the rear door for me. Not locking it. You said something then, but he rolled up the window so I couldn't be sure what. I can't say that you looked happy. But you didn't look surprised, either. And please tell him that your right brake light is out. He's good at fixing things.

Maybe it's personal shopping for land, like shopping for underwear. An intimate moment Kyle needed alone, with you. You want to let your guard down, relax and wear—or build—whatever your heart fancies, without being judged by others. But can I tell you something, Sheila? Plans change. What looks good on paper—or in the mirror—will never be the same again. I understand that you don't invite just anyone to look at where you'll be putting up walls and fences. Who you may want to let in, and keep out. What direction your driveway faces. Your waistline. These matters are private. But I was snowed in with nowhere to go. And I was out of coffee.

It's a slippery slope being angry at Kyle. Knowing I was laid-off from the *Almanac* for the winter, he located the cabin for me just as the forest service was threatening to raze them all. Tracked down the owner in Tucson, and helped write the lease. No one had ever wintered at this property. Kyle helped me put in a wood stove, and he chewed out the woodcutter good when he delivered that green mesquite. The smoke was awful. And then, my gosh, the smoke was good; the man had refused to give me a refund, but Kyle negotiated a compromise. The parcel the woodcutter left us made everyone happy for weeks. A slippery slope that, too.

Sheila, I like Kyle. You had told me that he appreciated you taking in his son, and that he could fix anything that was broken. That day last fall was special when the three of us climbed Mt. Wrightson, the thick scent of the towering Ponderosas so intoxicating that our legs seemed drunk and hardly moved us. The contrasting view of the arid Whetstone Mountains to the east was stunning. Kyle is an excellent guide, and I'm grateful for all that he has done for us both. So I guess he had his reasons this morning, leaving me standing in your driveway feeling stupid.

You know I've had better days, Sheila. Maybe it's the elevation. Or isolation. My thoughts are a mess, one is never in step with the other, they plunge and soar like the mountain itself; winter is cold above the desert floor. Quite the opposite of the heat our last summer in Michigan. Would Kyle even care about that? He's not the sort of man who looks in his rearview.

Sheila, this is awkward. When I was in town on my bike—after buying groceries at the Safeway and stuffing my panniers—I stopped at the Silver Peso for a beer before starting the long climb home. Inside it was dark and cool and quiet, same as always. The bar top looked dirty. Same as always. So I settled into a booth near the back exit, where I had left my bicycle. The front door opens and in walks Kyle hand-in-hand with that dark-haired woman that we once saw at the pharmacy. You had asked me then if I knew her. They now sat at the bar, and I edged closer to the wall of my booth so they couldn't see me. I heard plenty though. They weren't talking about the weather or property or the price of firewood. I'm sorry. It's a slippery slope, I know. I have now betrayed him and hurt you, and things will never again be the same for the three of us.

I am sorry, too, it's come to this. Leaving this note where Kyle will not find it. In that private place of yours. The shoebox under your bed with our letters, Sheila…

I had better get going up the mountain now. The sun is out, and with luck the road between us may open soon. A thaw is coming, they say.

Of Apples and Oranges

Sarita had dressed hastily, not wanting to miss her ride to the county building. Now she wiped the grime from the bathroom mirror there and stared at her reflection. Rough skin that the cold at the migrant camp had made worse. Eyes that once blazed with fury and defiance now resigned to watch others put out fires. Once she was the head of her class and, later, the first hired. Once. Now she had no job and little money and was asking for help. She applied a violet shade of lipstick to her cracked lips, tied her hair back and rejoined her son Jesse in the lobby that smelled of diesel, processed fruit and gutted fish. Those fish—huge salmon, taken from the weirs along the Stillwater River and slit open for their eggs—were actually processed up the street. When the day shift ended there workers came here to Human Services to apply for benefits, and the stink on their clothes and dull rubber boots was inescapable.

On this crisp October day, mother and son settled into the smells and into the waiting. Across the parking lot from the Bear County government building forklifts at Northland Cannery dug into pallets with their crates of apples. Sarita and Jesse watched them go back and forth from the loading docks to the idling trucks. Sunlight reflected off the steel blades and occasionally shot through the lobby's floor-to-ceiling windows marking a face here and there.

"You only put your hair up in the orchard," twelve-year old Jesse said. He stood up, sat down and got to his feet yet again, as if mere contact with the chair burned his skin. All bone and angles, Jesse did not sit well. "And you still owe me for two bushels," he added, shoving his hands into the pockets of his jeans.

"You'll get it on the bus," said Sarita. "When we go home." She picked at the hem of her dress, which reached the tops of her brown leather boots, a name brand that she found at the Goodwill after the squash.

They didn't need much during asparagus and pickles. Steady work. But now apples were over, and besides, after pickles Sarita had to pay rent because her farmer didn't grow apples. And so many workers in the orchard! Never enough boxes. She had just enough money for the bus home. But if she spent it—then what?

The receptionist called her name. "I can give you an appointment for tomorrow afternoon," she said, looking at an oversized book on her desk. "Or you can wait for a caseworker now."

Sarita looked out the window at the tops of the trucks brimming with apples, the name *Gray & Sons* stenciled on the crates. Maybe she helped fill this truck, she thought. She worked for Peter Gray, a veteran with a bad limp that worsened with the cold. The morning of the first frost, last week, he apologized to the crew for not getting out of his truck.

"I'll wait," said Sarita.

In time a door opened and a middle-aged woman said to follow her. Among the dizzying jumble of cubicles at Human Services that seemed to have fallen helter-skelter from the sky, hers was the neatest of the lot. Sarita squeezed Jesse's shoulder hard as she walked behind him, and his head swung toward her. A small and slightly askew crucifix as bright as bone hung from a partition behind the caseworker's desk. Sarita resisted the urge to straighten it. Mrs. Wilcox introduced herself and asked them to sit. The application was open on her desk.

"Did you go to the police about the car?" the caseworker asked. She wore a red business suit and her round face was framed by straight brown locks that fell in a perfect line to her jaw. Her skin was soft and unblemished.

Sarita pushed a loose strand of hair from her face and draped both arms around Jesse, holding him tight. "No," she said. "It was in his name."

"Whose name?"

"Berto's. A farmworker I met." She had needed money to send home, and he gave it to her in exchange for the title. When she paid him back, he kept the car and the money.

"Aren't you receiving child support?"

"The boy's father disappeared. Before he was born, in fact. The court in Hidalgo never did find him. I put that on the application too. Page 17," she added, and at once regretted doing so.

"You sure made some poor choices," said Mrs. Wilcox.

You don't know the half of it, thought Sarita. I made poor choices because the good ones were taken. The court knew where Jesse's father was; the prosecutor wouldn't bring charges. It was complicated. Sarita's father got some money from the man, which he used to pay her mother's hospital bills. Sarita had to be cautious about what she said. The caseworker could turn it around, make it sound like something you didn't mean. By then it was written down and later if you said something different or something more it would seem like you had changed your story.

Mrs. Wilcox worked at her computer. Sarita turned toward the voices from across the aisle. The welfare building was nothing more than a huge lighted box. Everyone heard everyone else's business.

"I don't like it here," said Jesse.

"We'll be on the bus tomorrow," said Sarita, stroking his hair.

"Does he have head lice?" the caseworker said, peering over her monitor. "It's going around the school."

"No," said Sarita, quickly withdrawing her hand.

"You had all season long to plan for the end of the harvest," said Mrs. Wilcox.

"Is that a question?"

"You're how old?"

"You have it there in front of you."

"Twenty-eight and you seem to be drifting without direction. Know what I mean? Lost. There's no money for this. Bus tickets. Didn't you go to Florida at this time last year to pick oranges?"

"It didn't turn out so good," said Sarita.

"Apples and oranges," said Mrs. Wilcox. "There's got to be something better."

Sarita thought of the trip north in April, and how even in the middle of nowhere the next state welcomed them with signs as big and bright as billboards. That is what the signs said. Welcome. To Oklahoma. Or Missouri. Illinois. Michigan. They drove an old sedan, avoiding the super highways, and often played a game to stay awake as one town or field dissolved into the next.

"Are we lost, mamá?" Jesse would say.

"We're not lost, *hijo*. How can we be lost with that sunken barn over there and that crooked stop sign next to the pasture plain as day and look at that rusty old bus with the weeds growing sideways out its windows? We've not come this way. It's all new." Miles later she might say, "*Dios mío!* It seems that we've been on this stretch of highway all our lives! Are we lost?"

"No! We're not!" Jesse would answer, pushing hard against his seatbelt. "Remember that old barn we passed, and the stop sign bent in half like an old man and the dumb bus? How could we be lost? We crossed the railroad tracks just once and the mighty Mississippi River just once and see that big silo rising to the clouds? It's all new, mamá. All new."

They tried to make the pieces of the journey theirs, each adding one more object—a place, a thing, a name—to this song of the road. Sarita thought that the two of them were perhaps like migratory birds, searching the hills and valleys below for a sign to stay on course. That simply staying at Jesse's side through thick and thin was a game that she could win. The day they left Texas and the day they'd return were bookends to the year, and she struggled not to call the space in between empty.

Now she heard the printer outside the cubicle, and her heart sank. It was a done deal. She looked past Mrs. Wilcox to the window facing the courtyard, where the ivy had turned crimson. The wind pushed an empty swing.

"Is something wrong?" said Mrs. Wilcox.

"I want to see the supervisor," said Sarita. *Es su derecho*, the poster in the lobby stated. It's your right. "I have to leave for Texas today or tomorrow. Apples are over. I'm out of cooking fuel." She pressed her hands on the caseworker's desk. "I have no money. The camp is closed, and my farmer asked me to leave. He said that he wasn't in the motel business."

"Why don't you call yourself Esperanza?"

Sarita felt the partition walls close in on her. It had been her mother's name, too. She shifted her weight uneasily in the chair.

"It says here that it's your given name. Esperanza Sara Madrigal. It's a pretty name."

"I don't want to," Sarita said. The pain nagged at her, like a rope burn; the years had given her some distance, but not slack.

"Well, we just don't haul off and call ourselves something different when things go bad, do we? Have you looked for a ride?"

"My friends…their cars were full," stammered Sarita. "They left already."

"Sadly, that isn't an *emergency*," said the caseworker as she tapped a large binder of manuals on her desk. "I'll tell the supervisor that you're here. You may wait in the lobby."

The application in her fist, Mrs. Wilcox stood, almost staggered, then hesitated. At that moment a loud noise, a backfire perhaps, shook the walls of the building. She looked across the aisle to the far windows that faced the highway. Sarita, by then also standing, followed her gaze: A steady stream of tourists travelled north for the fall colors, as trucks full of apples headed south to market. "Please," Mrs. Wilcox whispered. "I have to go. Something isn't right. You understand." Then Betty Wilcox, a plump forty years old and not looking well this day, said again, "It's a pretty name. I don't see why…"

Jesse made a face as Mrs. Wilcox walked away. "You put your hair up and wore the pretty dress for—"

"For you, *hijo*—"

"And look," Jesse said back. "Nothing."

It happens, she wanted to tell him. If nothing else, she wanted to teach him that. It happens. You want to please someone, a boss, or teacher maybe. A lover. The Creator. Government worker. It happens. You want to please someone and you want something, too. Simple math, she wanted to tell him. It just doesn't always come out even.

"I hate her," said Jesse. "*Que se vaya a chingarse.* And get hit by a car." He looked at his mother and grinned. Sarita slapped the side of his head.

Jesse sulked in the lobby, looking at a tattered *Sports Illustrated* as Sarita stood and read the posters on the wall: the upcoming harvest festival dance at St. Joseph's Church; the Indian Trails bus schedule (they would have to transfer in Berrien Springs); and a plea to report all child abuse and neglect. Her heart skipped a beat when she saw that. Maybe she shouldn't have slapped Jesse just now. He hasn't even gained back the weight he lost when he got sick after cherries, she thought. And did Mrs. Wilcox know that last week she kept him out of school two days to help with the apples?

Sarita continued to read each flyer, brochure and sheet, except one where the print had faded. She followed this paper trail around the room, past the children's pencil and crayon drawings until, startled, she came upon her own reflection. Some hocus-pocus or other trick, the hanging mirrored and magnified her every move.

She struck various poses as if trying on a new dress. At first the reflection only mimicked her, making her impossibly tall or—if she leaned just right—flat as a plank of wood.

"Jesse," she called out. "*Ven acá.* Look. It's magic."

"Then why don't you make that lady disappear," he said, without looking up.

Sarita returned to the fun-house mirror. Now there were two selves looking back at her: One razor-thin, like a small child, the other as big as a barrel. *Yes, two of me*, she thought. *Framed to order*. But what was it that she wanted? To move forward, or back? Up or down? Each direction had its moments, distortions and truths. As she watched herself in the glass she thought of times when grace and confidence crossed paths to flourish, however briefly, to provide her a buoyancy that barely left her feet touching the ground. It hadn't taken much: the small garden plot that her father left her to tend. The strawberries that she picked one season in Mears that the farmer let her sell at the roadside, the earnings fetching her school clothes for another year. Eighth grade graduation, when the class voted her the one most likely to succeed. She did that, all right: First in her class, and first to get pregnant. But she had fought to keep Jesse. The social workers said that he would have better opportunities elsewhere. Sarita said, better *things*? Schools? Doctors? Teeth? All of that, she knew. But a better love?

Sarita self-consciously glanced around the lobby. An older couple was trying on winter coats from a rack on wheels. A janitor mopped a corner of the tiled floor. Across from Jesse a handful of other clients chatted among themselves. A tall, slumping man, his back to her, stood waiting for the receptionist who was talking on the phone. No one paid attention to Sarita, and she was relieved.

She again looked into the mirror. The child started walking, yet not going anywhere, as alongside of her the barrel improbably bobbed and weaved like a balloon in space. Now the figures seemed to melt, like snow, and the screen went blank. The show was over, and Sarita breathed a sigh of relief. Time to rejoin Jesse, she thought, and wait for the supervisor. But as she turned away, and to her great horror, the glass seemed to shatter, and fragments filled the air around her. Sarita staggered backwards, her hands covering her face. Fireworks? She hadn't heard a sound, but saw these things, nonsensible images that stayed in sight much to her dismay. She was dazed, feverish, immobile. "Jesse!" she shouted from her knees, but the boy didn't respond. She wasn't even sure the word had left her lips.

"We'll say a prayer for you, child," the janitor said quietly, towering over her. Sarita saw the old couple in their new winter coats, standing alongside him in the mirror. The mirror which she saw explode. It was, however, intact, and smooth. She stood and leaned against the wall, trembling.

"Never mind that," the receptionist called over to Sarita, waving at the glass. "Something left over from the science fair at Bear Elementary." The receptionist smiled broadly at her, and only then did the mirror seem to lose its grip, and Sarita stepped away. "Ms. Stern will be with you in a few minutes," she added.

Sarita glanced at Jesse, still absorbed in a magazine. The entire wall now came back into focus for her, like a table of contents in large, bold print. She crossed over to the bulletin board. The circus came to town, and left. *The play A Doll's House* opened that weekend at the community college in Sears Harbor. Christmas tree workers wanted at Brandon Farms. A reporter for the local newspaper was looking for a housemate to share expenses. His name was Mark Silver, and he rented a farmhouse near Crystal Valley. Circling back, she again saw the blank page with the faded ink, its corners curled, the content whitewashed by too many sunny days. She stared at it nonetheless, as if expecting to see a sign, some sort of writing on the wall. But nothing had changed. And then she realized—in an instant—that it had. The script was hers to write. And this is what she wanted it to say: *Mother and son. Going places.*

***

Rebekah Stern was as thin and white as a stick of chalk, but spoke to Sarita in Spanish. She didn't have to sit at the edge of her chair. The edge of a cliff, it seemed, at times. "Please think it over," she said. "I'll talk to Mr. VanSlyke at Lakeshore Acres. He hasn't shut down his camp yet. We'll help you find more permanent housing later on."

"The bus leaves—"

"Staying," said Ms. Stern. "Settling-out. Leaving Jesse in school, and getting your GED."

Stay? Since infancy she had moved and moved, from oranges to strawberries to peppers, from onions to peaches, from the Gulf of Mexico to Grand Traverse Bay. In the atlas of her life, Georgia meant onions; Ohio, tomatoes; and Lake Michigan, apples. And snow. The office windows shook and the sky turned black with exhaust as the big trucks muscled their way up the road from the loading docks. She thought of her father when he was young and strong and traveled north to work, and how he let her keep the drops beneath the trees and what he got paid for them was hers. Some November mornings, before the sun climbed above the hills, the apples wore little painter caps of snow that her father, moving his ladder about, shook free. Ice water would trickle down her neck.

"It seems so, well, unsettling," Sarita said.

"Will you be getting unemployment?"

"Probably. Some." Peter Gray was good about that. She didn't know about her famer. If she filed, would he want her back next year?

"Please think about it," the social worker said. "I'll call on you tomorrow."

Sarita had always looked upon Lake Michigan as her own Continental Divide, a border where all streams moved irreversibly in one direction or the other. The great lake stood for that place, a sea really, at the end of the line. You were from Texas, or Michigan. Migrant, or resident. The two mixed like oil and water. *Stay?* Her pulse quickened, as if the word itself gave chase. She had heard of migrants who stayed north. They survived, like fish out of water. Hooked on welfare. And if they cut the line—take care! You might be worse off than before. *Stand on your own,* her father had told her. He was the first to help her read between the lines, and explain that a green light here meant take caution there. The first to show her how to wield a hoe, and when to pick.

Sarita listened to the falling leaves scratch at Rebekah Stern's window, turned to see them swirl halfway to the sky, and beyond the cannery and fairgrounds, far out over the bay, she saw whitecaps churn and lick the low dark clouds. She had heard that come winter the lake was like a leaky faucet, sometimes the snow never stopped, you couldn't do a thing about it, drip drip drip, until finally the sky burst like a pipe and your car might be buried for weeks. If you had one. *Stay?*

"We'll wait another day," she sighed to Jesse as they passed through the lobby to the exit. Sarita nodded to the farm workers she had met one harvest or another, and recognized Miguel Sandoval, a friend of her father's, slouched quietly against the wall. His face was weathered, with wrinkles like the deep furrows of a plowed field. Maybe she didn't explain enough to Ms. Stern how desperate she was to go home. To not worry about Jesse. *Stay*? The question reminded her of what they had asked each other as kids, migrating north from *El Valle*: Would you rather burn to death, or freeze? Funny, she now thought. Only two options then. Left unspoken was how to survive in the middle.

The two left the county building and crossed the parking lot. Revived by the crisp air, Jesse ran on ahead. Sarita followed and her shoulders sagged, as much from the weight of the harvest as from seemingly holding up the net to some endless game where others, the caseworkers, volleyed back and forth. An apple that she couldn't reach.

The late afternoon sun broke through the heavy clouds that sat over the bay. So bright was its glare that Sarita had to cover her eyes as she scanned the parked cars for their ride to the camp. Now a young man in a hardhat ran towards her, frantically waving his arms and shouting. She turned away to see if Jesse had circled back and saw someone helping Mrs. Wilcox into a car. None of it made sense.

"I didn't see him!" shouted the youth as he caught up to her. "Is he yours?" About 20 years-old, sweat seemed to pour down his smooth cheeks. Then Sarita realized they were tears.

She looked past him at the wooden crate tilted precariously on a forklift blade. A second hardhat with thick shoulders kneeled over a body, its legs folded awkwardly. Jesse. Sarita ran towards him. Blood from his pant leg, the same color of the spilled apples, seeped into the cracks in the pavement.

"I didn't see him," repeated the youth, following Sarita. "The sun…"

"She said that we're lost, mamá," Jesse tugged on her sleeve and tried to stand, before faltering, as unsteady as a new born colt.

"Don't talk *hijo*," said Sarita.

The heavyset man applied pressure to a deep gash above Jesse's right knee. He took the boy's hand from Sarita's sleeve, briefly squeezed it in the folds of his own, elevated Jesse's legs and then covered him with a blanket. "I'm sorry," he said to Sarita. "He'll be okay. The risk is shock."

Sarita looked away. Grey-black diesel from the trucks streaked the cold blue sky, and from above her on the cannery roof exhaust fans spit out the sticky smell of ripened fruit. She gagged, and waited for her breath to return. For the world to stop spinning.

"Talk to him," said the heavyset man. Sarita nodded and looked at Jesse, his face drained of all color.

"How can we be lost," said Sarita, "if the cannery is right here and the apples, look at all the apples! They knocked you over good! And the office we just left over there?" Her words came in swells, pushed up from the deep and unthinkable. "How can we be lost when I'm at your side? And this man with the first aid is helping you plain as day? How can we be lost..." But now the words caught in her throat. They seemed misguided, something that she had once drawn sustenance from, and now, with gut-wrenching effort, had to be kept down. She knew that it was no longer a matter of following a map and finding a signpost here, or river there. Words that once had amused the two of them she could not bear to say, or hear.

Yes, she wanted to cry out. *Yes*, hijo. *Lost. Lost to God.*

She blamed herself for not receiving child support. Losing her car. Heating the cold trailer with cooking fuel and then running out. Asking Mrs. Wilcox for bus tickets. For all the untold losses that had piled up and that had led her to this day and this minute to this godforsaken loading dock and that had tricked her into thinking there was something to gain. Migrating birds, she thought. What sign do they look for now? What song?

Still, she knew she must comfort Jesse. She kneeled, put her head alongside his and stroked his face. "Dear boy," she whispered. "How can we be lost with the sirens so close—hear them? We're not lost. We're not lost. We're not..." Her voice wavered. She smoothed back Jesse's patch of hair.

Trucks moving out from the loading docks stopped for the approaching ambulance. Their shift ending, workers trickled out the cannery doors, several stopping to watch Sarita. She stood, and looked down the road at the flashing lights and parting traffic. Suddenly, a path cleared for her as well. She saw through her self-recriminations and doubts. Understood that leaving them meant staying. Settling-out in Bear County. She was a good mother.

"Not lost," she turned and said to the workers, their bright yellow and steel hardhats like small constellations of suns. "The road ahead," she said, louder yet. "It's here."

Harvest Time

On his second day at the hospital Jesse saw Mrs. Wilcox, the caseworker who wouldn't give his mother bus tickets home. This was huge. He blamed her for being stuck in Michigan, and not on the bus to Texas. He wanted to pay her back. He didn't much care how that came about as he propelled himself on his crutches through the corridors of Lakeshore Memorial to his room that evening. He could only guess how good it would make him feel when it did. Once inside his room, he shut the door, closed the blinds and was about to grab his new white coat when his mother Sarita arrived.

He had drifted in and out of consciousness the first night, his dreams unspooling in endless loops of touchdown glory on his home field in Donna, Texas. His grandfather, mother and cousins cheered. He was soaring, moving effortlessly, scoring at will each time he touched the ball. Then in a flash the goalposts moved, and the faces he thought he knew changed. He felt himself to be in a hurry. To go where? The weight and the waiting were unbearable. Time passed. A nurse's mouth opened and closed and her words came from a different place than her lips. Jesse thought he cried out, but his own voice apparently went unheard. The nurse held something in her hand. Someone's wrist. His. He observed this from where he floated above his bed, looking down at the boy in it. Then—voices of men in gloved hands pulling a rope. Bells. A clanging of pots and pans. He felt terribly alone in this strange place, and he felt a giddiness, too, as the curtain slowly lifted and the light of a new day was upon him, casting yet another spell.

"Jesse," Sarita said, in his face, a hand on his forehead. She waited. "Jesse. The drugs put you out. Jesse?"

A nurse introduced herself as Marie. She was short and stout with a nest of curly dark hair. "Do you remember what happened?" she said. "Do you know where you are?" There was a gap in her upper front teeth and she whistled when she spoke. "The hospital," Marie continued. "Are you in pain?"

Jesse's leg was bandaged, his elbow pinned down by what felt like a nail running through it. "My head hurts," he finally said, with difficulty. "My arm, too."

Marie adjusted the IV attached there. She said that the emergency doctor had cleaned his leg, removing splinters left by the crate of apples. Nothing broken. He could have breakfast if he wanted. Or just a popsicle.

"When do we go back to Texas?" said Jesse. He thought of football, his grandfather, the skinny girl Alicia from Reynosa, who had waved goodbye to him in April.

Marie looked at Sarita. "The doctor closed part of the wound. You'll need more tests when the swelling is down, to see if there was nerve damage."

"Nerve damage," sighed Sarita, "is when you find your child on the pavement bleeding."

Marie said that the resident would look at the leg again soon. Then she'd change the dressing. The wound was draining. She asked Sarita if she needed a place to stay. Sarita said that Rebekah Stern from Human Services had found a family where she could live temporarily.

Sarita watched the nurse and an aide transfer Jesse into a wheelchair. "He's got to start moving," Marie said. "Even if just this." They kept his leg elevated. From her notes she read to Sarita what the emergency doctor said, as the aide finished positioning Jesse. "Forklift tore patient's flesh, above right knee. X-rays negative. Crush injury not ruled out . . . possible compression of muscle tissue." Marie indicated the IV and said that the doctor had ordered an antibiotic and anti-inflammatory along with a painkiller. The wound would have to be cleaned frequently. More stitches would be required. He got a tetanus shot, too.

"His shots are current," said Sarita defensively, reaching into her purse for Jesse's records.

"A precaution," said Marie. She asked Jesse to hold the IV pole, and Sarita wheeled him from the room.

After lunch a nurse with red hair cleaned the wound, changed the dressing and said that a specialist would examine him. She said that it was a miracle that his muscles, tendons, and blood vessels were not cut. Maybe he could go home soon. She removed the IV.

"I live in Texas," Jesse said.

The nurse provided crutches to Jesse, and the freedom to move on his own as long as the swelling continued to go down. Maneuvering came easy to him; his arms were strong from working in the orchard. Mr. Gray, the grower, had called him *podersoso ratón*, mighty mouse. Still, Jesse's leg gave him an uneasy feeling. At times his toes went numb. He wandered the corridors of the small two-story hospital when Sarita wasn't there, poking around the old building, finding doors locked and unlocked. He had visited a hospital once before, to see his grandmother. He remembered waiting for her to come home, but she never did. Now he used a crutch to push on an unlatched door, which opened to a bright closet-like room where crisp white coats hung wall to wall. He fingered one, a coat much like a doctor might wear.

"Go ahead," said Marie behind him. "Try it on."

"Were you following me?"

"To keep you out of trouble." He leaned on her as she put the crutches aside and helped him into the jacket. It reached his knees, but another nurse passing by said that he looked darling and insisted that he keep it on. She rolled up the sleeves to his wrists and pinned them. Jesse followed Marie to a desk where she wrote on a name tag, *Jesse Madrigal, Chief of Operations*, and stuck it to his lapel. "Your third day here," said Marie. "And already you're at the top of the heap." Jesse decided to hide the coat in his room, where Sarita would not find it.

Toward evening, as he catapulted himself past the nurses' station, Marie called out to him. "Sit, my dear friend, and listen to this." She read from the *Bear County Almanac*. "'It was the first accident at Northland Cannery in seven years, and—although the numbers are not in yet—the late season apple crop promises to be the best in a decade. The twelve-year-old migrant boy likely didn't hear the forklift above the din of the heavy trucks leaving the lot for market. X-rays were negative, and he has made many friends at Lakeshore Memorial.'" Marie looked up at Jesse. "Front page stuff. You're famous."

Jesse smiled and eyed the pizza box alongside her paperwork. Marie warmed up a piece for him. "Who told the newspaper all that?" he said.

"The reporter Mark Silver was here. He talked to me, and your mother. There isn't much else to report on in these parts."

"Do you like it that way?"

Marie was silent for a time. "Quiet is good," she said at last. "Not a stop light in the whole county. Or McDonalds. People come here to forget the places they leave. Vacation homes near Lake Michigan for some. Hiding out for others." She took the remainder of the pizza and walked off. When she didn't return, Jesse lingered for a few minutes.

That was about right, he thought. They'd left Human Services, he rounded a corner—and bam! Didn't see or hear the forklift. The pain was like a thousand bee stings. But he wondered why the reporter didn't ask *him*; talking to adults came easy to Jesse. He often translated documents for older workers in the orchards and fields, and phone calls to distant grandchildren who didn't speak Spanish. Other times he helped out at Peter Gray's office, explaining to workers deductions for this or that on payday. Probably the same reporter who had interviewed his mother after the squash, he thought. He seemed to like Sarita; a lot of men did.

Just then he heard the chirp of a siren. Jesse jammed his crutches hard into the floor, and swung himself over to a window across from the entrance to the emergency room. Outside, the hospital's bright lights cut into the falling dark, and the street was quiet. A few geese skittered along the pond on the hospital grounds as an ambulance came to a stop. A man and a woman in uniforms opened the rear doors and wheeled out a patient. And he saw her, Betty Wilcox, plain as day, and as helpless as a newborn. *Stupid lady*, thought Jesse. *We just wanted to go home.*

"A neighbor found her," a voice said, startling him. He turned to see an orderly, and wondered if he had followed him, too. "She'd fallen," the clean-cut young man said.

Jesse returned to his room. Seeing Mrs. Wilcox had set his heart pounding. He wondered if she'd stay at the hospital, and if so, where? He couldn't wait to ask her, *how are you feeling*? Of course, he'd be pretending. He didn't care how she felt. She was a whacko. And he'd say, *Wouldn't you rather be home*? Maybe then she'd get it. They had only asked for bus tickets to Texas. But just then Sarita's arrived, and interrupted his thoughts. She had heard from the doctor that his leg was draining well, she said, and the swelling was down. Her ride to the hospital waited outside now to take her grocery shopping. She'd be back soon as she could.

Jesse lay in bed with his leg elevated, trying to read *Animal Farm*, which his teacher had sent over. The words, however, seemed to jump all over the page; he had only one thing on his mind, and that was revenge. Now the wall behind him hummed. He grabbed his crutches and looked into the hallway, just as the elevator doors opened. The same orderly wheeled a patient on a gurney past his door. A couple and a younger man followed. Several rooms near Jesse's were occupied but never had visitors, and another room toward the end of the hall had been empty from day one.

It was there where Betty Wilcox was left.

Jesse waited, perched in his doorway. A short time later, he heard the visitors leave Mrs. Wilcox's room. "She doesn't get it," the younger man said. "She'll be okay," said the older one. "I'm worried," said the woman, as the three disappeared in the elevator.

The hospital floor was laid out like a small "t," with the nurses' station at the cross, and usually deserted after eight o'clock. Seeing no one, Jesse now slipped on his white coat and quietly propelled himself down the hall. He peered into the caseworker's room, surprised that it was smaller than his own. Mrs. Willcox lay in bed, a patch over one eye, a bruise on her forehead. He hopped closer. Her hair that was perfectly combed when she interviewed them in her office wasn't so perfect anymore. She appeared to be asleep, her frail torso attached to a spiderweb of cords and tubes. *Like a helpless bug*, thought Jesse. He leaned over her bed for a moment and thought, too, that he might free her, using his crutch like a magic wand to make all the wires and such that protruded from Betty Wilcox—along with herself—disappear. He watched the blinking of the monitors that she was connected to, the only bright things under the dim light.

The caseworker opened her one eye.

"Are you the resident? Please. Are you?" She stared out from her loose bedsheets like a anxious child afraid of what goes bump in the night. "I don't want to go to Grand Rapids to see the neurologist," she said, grabbing the hem of Jesse's white coat. "I don't want to see anyone. Please," she said, again. Jesse marveled at this small, plump fist that held fast to his borrowed coat. He thought it marvelous, too, that this woman who he blamed for his family's troubles was now so in need herself.

"What is it?" he said nervously. "What do you want?"

"Please, doctor. I can't do this anymore."

For the first time Jesse understood the significance of the coat he wore. He thought of tossing it in the corner, and running. If he could. But he only removed the woman's hand, leaned back on his crutches, puffed his chest out, and said: "Is this an emergency, Mrs. Wilcox?"

"Yes, I suppose it is."

"An *eh-mer-hencia*," Jesse said slowly, pronouncing the word in Spanish and then parroting the words Mrs. Wilcox had used at her office, "is something unforeseen, something that you can't predict."

Mrs. Wilcox said that she wasn't feeling well. She didn't understand.

"*No hay emergencia!*" Jesse said. "You had your whole life to get better. And not be the person you are." He wasn't sure why the words came out that way. Hearing them reminded him of the feeling he had when he was looking down at himself that first night at the hospital; it was, and wasn't him. He didn't know what to believe, then or now, and was overcome by sorrow. For his messed-up leg, and all the touchdowns he wouldn't score in Pop Warner. For not being able to wrestle his grandfather. For not being on the bus home. For Betty Wilcox, and wanting to tear from her what he thought she'd taken from him.

Mrs. Wilcox wet her lips with her tongue. She squinted out of her one eye, and raised her arm as if to block the little light there was. "Are you my doctor?"

"I am Jesse Madrigal. You wouldn't give us bus tickets home."

"I don't want to go on like this," said Betty, looking away. "Help me."

Bingo! thought Jesse. He gleefully imagined the reporter's next headline: *It was the first accident at the county hospital in seven years . . .*

"What do you need?" asked Jesse.

"Bring me that bag." Jesse didn't move. "Over there. On the chair," she said, in a tone—even in her weakened state—reminding him of her office and everything he didn't like about her. "My purse," Mrs. Wilcox said.

Jesse turned to the chair by the window. On the sill above it he saw a vase of strawberry-colored roses, and a card, which was open. *Mother, Come Home*, it said. He hesitated.

"I didn't ask for flowers," said Mrs. Wilcox.

Jesse brought her the bag, and she told him to empty the contents on her bed. She took a container of pills but lacked the strength to open it. Standing on his good leg, Jesse reached over to unscrew the cap, and then emptied the vial into her shaking hand. *This is what she wants*, he thought, and smiled. But he thought, too, of what his grandpa would tell him: *If you truly think misery loves company, then you don't know what hurt is.* His heart that was so full of purpose and vengeance only a moment ago was now teeming with emotions that he didn't understand.

As Mrs. Wilcox went to swallow the pills, Jesse gently laid his left crutch on her arm to prevent her from raising it. "Please," he begged, leaning forward and wrapping her hand in his. "Let me get you some water."

Betty Wilcox nodded.

Jesse instead pushed the call button on her headboard with the tip of the crutch, then seated himself on the bed alongside her.

"Doctor," she said. "Can I swallow these?" Minutes passed and still Jesse sat there, griping her hand in his. He listened for footsteps but only heard the drone of the machinery she was hooked up to, and her short, rhythmic breaths.

"It's not a good idea, Mrs. Wilcox," said Jesse finally.

A tall nurse who he didn't recognize walked into the room. "What are you doing here?" she said. "And where did you get that coat?"

"Marie said that—"

"Marie doesn't work this shift," said the nurse. "Take it off. Now."

"Look—" Jesse said and he opened his trembling hand to show the nurse Mrs. Wilcox's, still clenching the pills.

"Did she swallow any?"

"No," said Jesse.

The nurse looked closely at the pills, took them from Mrs. Wilcox—who offered no resistance—then raised the bed and checked her vital signs.

Jesse had felt like a superhero when he put on the white coat. *Chief of Operations!* All that was missing was a cape, and boots. Not chief, he now thought. *Stupidman.* He laid the coat on the chair, and glanced at Mrs.

Wilcox. Before leaving the room, and still determined to exact something from her, with the nurse's back to him, he took a rose from the sill.

He met his mother coming down the hall, and gave her the flower.

"Where did you get it?" Sarita said, pleased.

"Mrs. Wilcox."

"Oh! Did I miss her?"

"No, she's here. Sick."

"And she gave you this?" Jesse was silent. "*Hijo?*"

"I wanted something from her," Jesse said. "So I took it."

"Then you'll have to give it back."

They turned to Mrs. Wilcox's room, but the door was closed. Sarita laid the rose on a stand outside it. She gave Jesse a pen. On a paper napkin, he wrote: *Mrs. Wilcox, I took the flower and I'm sorry. I hope you go home soon. Jesse Madrigal.*

"The doctor said that we could leave tomorrow, if the tests are okay," said Sarita. "They'll sew you back up and send us on our way."

"Texas?"

"I found a place for us here. A farm near Crystal Valley. I think you'll like it. You'll need follow-up appointments and physical therapy. I already scheduled some. I'm going to take classes, and work at the cannery. Your Aunt Teresa in Chicago is loaning us the money to buy a car."

Jesse didn't sleep well that night. He didn't hallucinate, or remember dreaming anything. When a nurse entered his room in the wee hours of the morning to ask if he was alright, he did not look her in the face. "I'm fine," he said, defiantly.

After breakfast they wheeled him into a different wing. A doctor examined him, determined there was no nerve damage or infection, then closed the remainder of the wound. Sarita packed up the few things from his room. They were waiting for their final instructions when Amber—the nurse who had confronted Jesse in Mrs. Wilcox's room—brought a different wheelchair, explaining that hospital policy required every patient use one upon discharge. And no, Jesse couldn't keep it, only the crutches until his mother arranged for his own. Amber then asked them to follow her down the hall.

"Is this about the insurance?" Sarita asked. Amber said only, "You'll see." When she opened an unmarked door past the nurses' station, a roomful of hospital staff stood up to applaud Jesse. Marie presented him a cake in the shape of a football with blue and silver frosting. Dallas Cowboy colors.

"For our young hero," announced Amber. "You likely saved a

patient's life."

Sarita, beaming, looked at Jesse, who burst into tears and quickly wheeled himself out of the room, thanking God that the door had been propped open.

Sarita found him minutes later down the corridor looking out the window over the duck pond. "Jesse—" She put a hand on his still heaving shoulder.

"Mrs. Wilcox wanted to end her life," Jesse said, catching his breath between sobs, not turning around. "And I wanted to help her do that."

The two watched a young boy on the hospital grounds jerk his arm skyward. They saw a stone launch high in the air that in a blink of an eye flitted across their window, like a birdwing. The bright stone plunged downward, breaking the smooth surface of the pond, the ripples reaching the marshy grass some yards away. Sarita pulled Jesse close.

Snow Country

Mark Silver peered through his truck's windshield this snowy December afternoon, trying to find his way. Whiteouts swept over the pickup and he floated, a cloud among clouds, pulled forward blindly as if to a hitch in a carwash. When the snow finally let up he turned off the radio ("Do You Hear What I Hear") and stepped outside to figure out where he was. *At least I'm on a road*, he thought, seeing the misty outline of trees only yards from his truck door. He drove on cautiously, passing bleak fields of what had been corn or squash, and not until he climbed a steep hill above the town of Sears Harbor did he know the road he travelled. Winter was like that along the Lake Michigan shore—at times you needed a plow or snowmobile, maybe both—but the skiing was good, and Mark thought that if what was good was also important in your life, then you were well off.

He wandered in and out of the aisles at the market, grabbed a few things, and chatted with the cashier before walking slowly back to his truck. Town smelled of cut pine, road salt, and gasoline from the handful of snowmobiles squatting in front of Walker's Bar. Vendors selling wreaths and trees mostly ignored Mark and that suited him just fine. Here and there, he heard the scrape of a shovel and the splitting of wood. The bells from St. Vincent's Church tolled softly in the fog of snow. Small lights burned from storefront awnings, blinking like portholes in vast and snow-covered hulls. Afternoon soon faded into dusk.

"Silver. Merry Christmas. Got your tree up?" Eddie Brandon, who ran his family's Christmas tree farm, startled him.

"No, guess I don't," Mark said.

"I got one for you. About giving them away at this point." Eddie was short with a sharp beak for a nose and he stood there in his Carhartts without hat or gloves, snow filling his shaggy blond hair and beard like fine sugar.

Mark looked at the fir trees leaning against the hardware store, which the Brandons also owned. They seemed freakish to him, limp and meager. "Not this time," he said. "But thanks."

"Hell and tarnation, Silver, how do you do without a tree? You leaving town?"

Mark shook his head.

"Then I'm giving you one. I know you ain't working now." He went to grab a tree. "Where you parked?"

"Ah, thanks again. But same answer."

"Silver! Unless you cut your own, you won't find a better deal. It's free. Free!"

Mark shifted the weight of his bag. Eddie, however, misunderstood the gesture, and thought Mark was handing him the groceries to carry the tree himself.

"I can take that for sure," said Eddie, reaching for the bag and giving Mark the tree.

"Please," said Mark. "I don't want it."

Eddie put the tree down. Beads of ice were frozen to the ends of his eyelashes, stuck there like spider eggs. "I don't get it. You one of them Je—"

"—Gypsies?" said Mark, his throat tightening.

"Yeah, Gypsies," Eddie said, nodding.

"Something like that," said Mark.

"I'll be," said Eddie. "The whole family?"

"As long as I remember."

"That so?" Eddie said, his blue eyes probing Mark's face. "We'll say a prayer for you." He shook his head and turned his back to look up the street.

Mark got back to his truck and exhaled. Leaving Sears Harbor, he followed a county plow until it turned on the state highway to Stillwater. He was on his own. The snow fell in great strips now, like pieces of ragged linen, and his wipers, lurching back and forth, screeched into the quiet, trying to make a difference. Fifty yards from the house he lost control of the truck, slid harmlessly into a drift by the creek, and from there had to go on foot. The snow was deep, but light, and he followed a deer trail until it cut back into the woods. Sarita waited for him on the porch, snow like stardust in her long black hair.

"Do you need help carrying it?" she asked. She started to call for her son Jesse but stopped. She knew. "You don't have it," Sarita said. "Will you be going back out?"

"Can't see a thing out there," said Mark. He brushed himself off and carried the one bag of groceries inside. She followed him to the fireplace, where he tossed in a chunk of wood, and busied himself arranging the logs just so. Mark knew little about Christmas trees, even less about the wanting of them, but he had found solid reasons for rejecting those that were left. Free or not. "They weren't any good," he said.

"I'm glad you're back safe," said Sarita. "Safe isn't the same as okay, is it?"

"I'm fine," Mark said, not turning around, mashing the logs about and staring at the rising flames. One lie fueled the next. "There's time. You'll see."

"Time for what?" she said.

Twelve-year old Jesse stood at the top of the stairway. The angle gave strength to his slight frame.

"It isn't so bad," said Mark.

"The weather? It's worse than bad," Sarita said. "It snows every day here." She grabbed the fire poker and playfully nudged him. "Or did you mean Christmas?"

Jesse raced down the stairs. "Why didn't you bring a tree?"

"Does it matter?" asked Mark.

"What do you mean?" said Sarita.

"Christmas goes on, doesn't it? Do you really need lights and trees and all that stuff?" He didn't mean for it to come out that way. He went to the window and watched it fill with snow, like an hourglass with sand. He shut his eyes tight, and still it came down. Christmas made him want to burrow underground like a mole, and come out when it passed. Mark Silver had always looked upon the holidays as King Solomon did upon the bereaved and contentious mothers: You go for one or the other. You had to shake the pretender out. What made him think that he could go buy a tree and celebrate Christmas?

He had left Sears Harbor with odds and ends, not with what he told Sarita and Jesse he'd bring home—today, yesterday, and for the past two weeks. Silver, thirty-two years old, had plenty of time these days. He was laid off from the *Bear County Almanac*, where he reported agricultural news and events; farmers didn't have much to say in winter. This last trip to town he'd gotten back to the pickup with his heart pounding—and he didn't even know what he had paid for. Now the snow came down faster than the plows could push it back, and the road would be drifted shut. Going back would be impossible, maybe for days.

"Why!" The boy repeated, circling Mark as if he were prey. For a time the three of them had lived in one of those snow-white paperweight worlds. Only now he wished someone would just stop shaking it.

"Jesse! Enough." Sarita steered him out of the room. He stepped around her. "We always have a tree!" Jesse yelled. "At least we used to." He added something in Spanish and his mother said to stop that right now.

"Jesse doesn't think he'll get anything without a tree," said Sarita, returning.

But they knew better. Gifts had come, from the great aunt and cousins in Chicago, her father and sister in Donna, Texas. The boy even signed for one himself. And with his first unemployment check, Mark had bought Jesse skis—not new ones, but used wooden ones that smelled of pine tar and wax and still had slow turns in deep powder left in them. He'd given them to the boy the first good snow after Thanksgiving.

Mark and Sarita stood face-to-face, loosely holding hands. She was almost as tall as his six feet, with broad shoulders and a darkly handsome face that her easy smile filled. Her eyes were black pools of resolve or devotion or desire—Mark was never sure which. She wore two pairs of jeans to keep warm (the second ones, the overalls, were his), and a wool sweater from the Goodwill. She smelled of coarse soap, not perfume, and fresh cut apples—the same as when he had interviewed her at the hospital for the *Almanac*, after Jesse's accident outside the cannery. She told him then her real name was Esperanza, but to call her Sarita. She said that she had stopped using Esperanza when her mother died. He reported that, too.

His articles about the hard work and hard knocks of the road-weary migrant mother and son were picked up by the AP wire. After the story—and harvest—ran its course, he offered them a place to stay.

"Farmers say that all the time," she had said.

"What do you tell them?"

"That my work is in the field. And stays there. If you want something more, go to Fred's List."

"I think you mean *Craigslist*," said Mark.

"Fred or Craig. You see what I mean."

"I'm not a farmer," Mark told her. "But I grow things just the same, and put them down on paper." He thought of the stories and novel that he would write during his layoff.

"So how many families does this paper of yours feed?" she asked.

He didn't have an answer then, and he didn't have one now.

Over her shoulder, in the yard where the kitchen lights fell, was a sea of white. Night came swiftly in the woods beyond. Mark yearned to join the storm outside, stark forests, heavy squalls, snow so frequent it never soiled. The world of black and white that he knew best. He squeezed her hands and turned away.

Sarita unpacked the groceries: flour, coffee, bagels, soy milk, shampoo, the *Detroit Free Press*. She already had what they needed to make a special dinner. "You go for a tree and bring this?" Her words were not unkind. They never were. "What were you thinking?"

"That I don't celebrate Christmas," Mark said. He saw Jesse's face in the doorway.

Sarita said nothing.

Mark went to the window—five inches of snow or twenty, what did it matter to her? After the first two her old beater car with the bad tires never got her anywhere anyway. But he would give her the truck if she wanted to leave. She knew that. When the lake first gave up the heavy clouds, they stayed up nights talking as the squalls drifted inland, wave after wave of snow that by morning clung like thick cotton to the black willows that surrounded his rented farmhouse. She told him that in Texas the heat came so fast and early in the year that those going north were considered lucky. But staying past fall? Unlucky. But maybe, just maybe, okay, she had said, smiling at him. She was taking classes, preparing for her GED, and would stay at least until Jesse finished his physical therapy. On Mark's first day home on layoff he overheard her talking on the phone. "*No es amor, ni el ambiente, ni Mark Silver,*" he thought she said. Her words echoed loudly in the large house and his heart sank, though he wasn't sure of the Spanish. "It's a good house," she said in English. "Colder than *El Valle* but warmer than the migrant camp." Of course it would be nice to be home for Christmas, she said. But they would see what it would bring, winter in this place.

Now the phone rang. Sarita, expecting a call from Texas, answered and passed it to Mark.

"Who was that?" his mother asked.

"Sarita. A friend."

"That's an odd name."

"Not around here."

His mother hesitated like a car caught between gears. Mark sensed that she wanted to go somewhere, say something, but was stalled. He pictured her in her red leather jacket, its collar turned up against the cold, surrounded in Detroit by dry pavement yet trying hard to steer clear of drifts of one sort or another. "What happened to the nice woman you wrote about?" she finally said. "Did she make it home?"

"Sarita and her son are staying at the farm. We're snowed in."

"Oh," she said, as if nothing had been said at all. "Will you be coming home soon?"

"It's a long way back, mother," Mark said.

***

Mark slept poorly that night. He moved from dream to dream, treading here, pushed there, each step closer to a side he could sense and never reach, as if he were crossing a fierce river without return.

Snow filled his bedroom with sand.

He saw his mother, lurching in that space between gears.

Voices scratched at his window, like sleet.

He was frightened and tried to run but his blankets gathered like drifts, pinning his ankles down. He saw himself at Sarita's door. The snow fell all around him now, and he called out to her. *If only I had my skis.* Then he was flying, really flying, carving turns around the black holes and bright constellations of his dream. He skied the planets and the stars, the sun and the moon, and along the Milky Way. But suddenly in this frenzy of space the snow gave way to ice, he lost control and plunged head over heels, his face peeled back like a mask on the barren, windswept slope. He got up, fell, and rose again, each time with a new face, a new mask. Finally, he stayed upright and brushed himself off. He wasn't hurt, but something was wrong: He could not find his way back. In anger, he raised his fist to the heavens. And the stars with their thousand faces laughed. Again he called her name. Esperanza.

Fully awake, Mark dressed and went outside into the night. The wind had shifted away from the lake, and with it the storm's fury. As the last of the dark clouds overhead broke up, the new snow glittered like diamonds. The cold that braced him failed to still his doubts. How did you give, without giving up? He listened to the now swollen creek that ringed the farm, as if an answer could somehow be plucked from it.

The snow was deep but light. The skiing would be very good. The only sounds were his heart and the quickness of the creek. Across the pasture and above the tall spruces by the highway, the gay lights strung on Miles VanSlyke's silo twinkled like distant stars.

He got the skis out, brushed himself off, reentered the house, and climbed the stairs. He tiptoed into Sarita's room and leaned over to kiss her. "*No, hombre,*" she protested, drawing the blankets to her forehead. "Your nose is like an igloo."

"You mean icicle."

"The same."

"I'll be back before sunrise. Jesse, too." He went to the door.

"Mark?"

"Yes."

"It's just a tree. Nothing has to grow from it."

"Is that what you want?"

"I don't know."

He shut her door, and awoke the boy.

"Now?" Jesse asked. "Why can't you go yourself?"

"Because I'm snow blind," said Mark, laughing.

"What's that?"

"When you know where you're going, but can't see the way there."

Downstairs, Mark warmed some milk and tucked Jesse's pant cuffs into a second pair of socks before the two laced up their ski boots. He put a thermos of hot chocolate, extra mittens, and a small folding saw into his pack.

It was new to Jesse: the squeaking hardness of the soft powder underfoot; the clapping and clacking of the sticklike box elders overhead, shaking free their slight burdens of snow; and the drum-like roll and thud of tall drifts sliding off the barn roof as the two skiers glided past. From a fence post an owl screeched at them and startled Jesse. Mark's heart also beat wildly.

After a mile they turned north, climbed several hills, and from the highest saw the tree farm below, where rows of pine tops bobbed above the thick snow like strings of dark beads. Buoyed by the deep powder, they skied fast and effortlessly downhill, and through the jammed open and partially buried gate.

Jesse picked a good one and they made quick work of taking the tree. Shuffling back under the arched gateway, the boy flicked a ski pole so quick and high at the overhang that he caught Mark off guard, showering his face with snow. Jesse howled with delight, then pointed overhead to the now exposed wrought iron sign that the snow had hidden. "Brandon Brothers Tree Farm," he read. Mark stopped. The excitement he felt only a moment ago was gone. He put the tree down.

"What are you doing?" said Jesse.

Mark jabbed at the sign with his pole. "I know these people."

"You said that there was no one. Nobody owned it."

"I thought it was abandoned. And it may be so. Thing is, Eddie Brandon tried to give me a tree in town yesterday. He got ticked off when I said no."

"But wouldn't he want you to have one then?"

"I don't know," said Mark. "Wanting to give, and then having the same thing taken from you are different." Giving was satisfying, he thought. It repeats, and redeems the gift of life. Taking undermines all that.

Jesse turned his skis so that he faced Mark. "Let me explain something to you, *Señor Serioso*," he said, barely able to contain his glee. "We can't exactly glue it back on now, can we?" The two skiers laughed heartily.

"Eddie Brandon, this be the one!" Mark shouted into the stillness of the night. "Thank you for keeping me in your prayers." He threw a chunk of snow at Jesse, who nimbly avoided it.

Mark lashed the tree to his ski poles to carry over his shoulder. He and Jesse switchbacked up the big hill, traversing and kick-turning until, reaching the tall pines, they could look out toward the great lake and see below all the farms and orchards nestled in the checkered folds of the snowy woods. The climbing was difficult—all the more so without the use of his poles—and though Mark's lungs burned, wood smoke from someone's hearth sweetened the cold air. Above them the stars stretched from horizon to horizon.

The wind picked up, so they took shelter behind a copse of pines bent in half by the weight of snow. Mark set the tree down, poured the hot chocolate, and the two skiers removed their sodden mittens to warm their hands on the steaming cups. Mark told Jesse there was probably more snow overhead in these trees than on the ground in all the cities downstate. He pondered a world that winter made smaller, humbler, and more primitive. Snow redeemed the fallowed land, made the harsh angles—the frozen, mudded ruts in the road, the downed limbs in the apple orchards, the debris of errant hunters—soft again, and skis were wings to explore it.

Jesse thanked him for the best hot chocolate ever, ducked under the snowy boughs and pushed off.

Mark tightened the small tree to his poles, shifted the weight over his shoulder and, steadying it with one hand, followed. Soon he heard the soft parade of deer moving into the swamp below. Living in the country, he often saw or heard what others—Sarita and Jesse, even—had to imagine. Then, too, he thought, at times—serious times—he was only able to imagine what they saw plain as day. Christmas, for example. Family.

Mark skied Jesse's tracks along the ridge, and then followed them down, down, leaning back on his heels so the tree wouldn't slip forward and cause him to catch his tips in the snow. He gained speed, faster and faster, finally slinging past the boy—only to skid to a stop near a candescent figure on the windblown crust at the edge of a cornfield. Jesse caught up and he, too, stared at the peculiar shape the wind and snow had slashed and carved and fused of withered stalks the combine had missed. Starlight danced in waves across it.

"What is it?" asked Jesse.

A *freak of nature*, thought Mark. Its single trunk and sweeping columns looked familiar, like a remnant from his past that, inexplicably, the storm had uprooted. Then he knew. "A menorah."

"A what?"

"A menorah. It's how my family—my people—honor their past. Lighting candles. Singing songs." Mark stared at the candelabra-like object that glowed between them until he started to shake. It was a festive holiday, he thought; had he forgotten that, too? And yet, away from the temple—skiing the dunes and woods—he had never felt closer to it. *But closer to what?* The question nagged at him. God was never his thing. Yet he undeniably felt closer and closer to...as if he were sliding downhill and couldn't stop the approach to something he had no name for. It pulled at him, this uneasy connection, like the pull of a former lover, the string never severed. He thought God was maybe that. A string without end.

Jesse knocked the ice from his skis with his pole. Mark wanted to say something that the boy would remember. "My father wanted to be a cantor," he blurted, as the tree fell to the ground.

"What's that?"

"A priest, sort of. Who sings."

Jesse shifted his weight to his stronger leg. "You don't celebrate Christmas."

"No." Mark stood the tree upright in the snow next to the candelabra.

"But why not, you know, be part of it? We're all people."

We're all people, thought Mark. Skiing the black holes, jumping from star to star. Skating the thin ice. "A long time ago, there was a fork in the road," he said at last. "The path my people took led me here."

"My mom says the past is past."

Mark laughed. His mother had told him that the past will never let you forget. "This is different," he said. "What I'm saying is, I can't go a way I've never been. I'd miss out on where I was. Who I am."

"So Christmas makes you feel, I don't know, like you turned the wrong way or something?"

"Yeah," said Mark. "Lost."

Jesse put his hand in Mark's, as much as his pole let him. "That was fun. I never skied like that. Didn't think I could do it."

"I never thought I could either," said Mark. He reached into his pack, got the scraper out, and shaved the ice from their ski bottoms. "We've got to move," he said. "Our skis are icing up."

"I don't get it," said Jesse, not going anywhere. "You find both—" he pointed to the tree and bundle of stalks. "And celebrate neither." He smiled at his own cleverness. "What do you believe, anyway?"

"That the sun will soon rise, as it should. So we'd better get going, get the firewood in and put the tree up."

What did he believe? That the earth embraced the sky. Simple. He believed in the stars and dreams and in certain waxes for certain days. He believed in magic where snow fell from a cloudless sky, and in castles made of ice stacked along the shore of the big lake on a sub-zero day and in the waves that made them and erased them and crashed over them to freeze in midair and shatter like glass. He was wet and chilled to the bone and it didn't matter. He believed that, too.

They were almost home: a last hill to traverse, then down and along a tangle of new growth where they'd find their old tracks. At their side, a few corn stalks not buried in the snow fluttered in the wind, and to the west, a black tongue of cloud welled up over the lake to swallow the last of the stars. The darkness behind the light. It would snow again.

The Return of Everything

I'm in the city to see family and pick up supplies at Brodsky's General Store. An older woman is returning an outdoor lounge chair. "I have one at home just like it," she tells each of us in the checkout line. "I don't need two of them."

Eyebrows rise like a curtain. She is looked at with suspicion; it's already fall, and the days left for outdoor gatherings are few. Another customer—I don't see who—tells her to keep it for company anyway.

"I don't get any," the old woman answers.

A man, thin like a stick of gum and wearing a stylish suit, scarf, and fedora joins the line and greets her.

"Hello, Mrs. Goldberg! Danny, Gertrude's son. Remember me?"

"No!" the old woman shouts. "And not that slut mother of yours, either."

There is an audible shuffling of feet. The line of customers lengthens, but not with more shoppers; she is being given space. In the quiet that follows, perhaps only seconds, I hear Elvis Costello on the PA. Traffic outside. A large truck. A horn. A siren in the distance.

Danny laughs, busies himself rearranging the items in his cart and wishes her well.

"*Nu?*" the old woman says to to him the ten or so of us waiting. "How well is that, shlepping this?" She adds that she's tired and has a bus to catch.

"Why don't you sit down on that thing and rest?" suggests another man at the front of the line.

"I don't want to use it," she answers, and grips the chair with both hands, holding it erect.

"*Bubeleh,*" the man says, studying her and the chair. "It looks used to me." He grabs his purchase and exits.

The woman then turns to me for an opinion. I start to look away, but not before I see a small burn hole in its orange webbing where the chair folds. I also see Judi Soberman standing in line a few places behind me, her back slightly turned. I want to hide. A large man buying lighter fluid and a jumbo package of white socks stands between us. I make myself small.

"It's like new," the old woman says, watching me.

Judi sees me, and half-smiles. "Mark Silver," she says. "I didn't know you were here." She's been crying. Her father is sick, she adds quietly. She needs me, I think. Seven years since I last saw her, at the time of my own father's death. She held me tight then, but when I called her over the weeks that followed—nothing.

I tell her that I'm sorry, and we turn to our places in line.

Before coming shopping, I visited my mother. She claimed Brodsky's went out of business. "I'm certain of it. It was in the *Jewish News,*" she said, shaking her head. "Old man Brodsky died. None of the kids had any interest in the place. Stock was piled everywhere like garbage. All of it a mishmash of times gone by."

"Or of times to come," I said, and she laughed.

My mother laughed often, yet rarely smiled. I took off my jacket. The slider to the balcony of her second story apartment was open, yet the heat was on. I knew these things were connected: her razor-thin comfort zone, and her abiding effort to not tip the scale one way or the other. Her maddening habit of demanding a restraint from others that she rarely heeded herself. The head-back, deep-throated laughter, and the singular inability to smile freely. The draft, and the furnace.

"The store isn't safe," she told me, which seemed preposterous. "They don't sell things. They loan them, they break, and you bring them back." She started to discuss her will, determined not to leave one cent more to one child than the other. I said that I hadn't come to discuss her will.

"You want it should go away?"

I didn't answer. Our conversations were often like that: long pauses surrounding a few words left exposed, like bits of land in open water. Neither of us was ever in a rush to jump in.

"You do not get things back in this world," she finally said, touching my wrist. "You just move on." Then she added, "That place has gone to the dogs. You'll end up with something you didn't ask for."

But I've wanted Judi since high school.

The cashier asks the old woman if anything is wrong with the chair. "It's like new," she says, handing him a crumpled receipt. He counts out the refund into her right hand. She tries to fold the bills, but is resigned to stuffing them in a pocket. She then lingers, clinging to the chair with hands like gnarled roots of a tree. "I know you're busy," she tells the cashier, "while I have nothing to do but wait for the bus. I'll put the chair back. Aisle eleven, below the cat food."

She seems friendless and lost. I'd like to put the chair back for her but don't want her to bite my head off, like she did to Danny. At least she has bus fare, I think.

"You have a nice day," she says to me, carrying the chair away.

"Don't miss your bus," I tell her.

I'm at the front of the line now. The man with the lighter fluid and white socks has disappeared, and Judi is behind me. In eleventh grade journalism class I watched her dot the *i* in her name with a small heart, and mine about stopped. We went on a date my senior year. I remember nosing my father's Olds into the theater parking lot, and the relief I felt taking up only one space. I remember how frightened I was when Judi leaned in close, the popcorn spilling. I remember the movie we saw. But not the perfume she wore, or the taste of her lips. Needing someone was a fearsome thing in my family, so I kept my business, my loneliness, to myself, and tried to become self-sufficient. And this is where that's gotten me: to Brodsky's, shopping for needs I cannot fill. To whispering sweet nothings alone into my bathroom mirror at night, and reaching for whatever pills are within. When I can't sleep, I go outside—I live in the country, in the middle of nowhere—to watch the stars, and when I see one fall, I think *that's the life for me*. Something more, even if it must fall from the sky.

"Is there anything else?" the cashier asks as he rings up my orange juice, pasta, new frisbee, band-aids, and flannel pajama bottoms (the package was open, and marked down).

Plenty, I think. I pay and wait for Judi outside. The autumn sun, low and harsh, reflects off a signpost at the curb making it difficult to see ahead as we walk in silence toward her car.

At the sign, a bus stop, the old woman is sitting and smoking a cigarette in the chair I thought she had returned. "The Silver Line," she says to us, without looking up. *Does she know me?* I'm confused, until Judi points to the signpost. It's the name of the bus route. Just then the wind catches Judi's hair, makes it swirl upward like an eddy of leaves. Her car is close and there is little time. The bus approaches.

I'm standing with a bag of goods, and a shopping list of regrets. I tell Judi of our imagined lives together. "All these years apart," I blurt, "empty like those black spaces between the stars."

She smiles.

"Remember the spilled popcorn?" I ask, as I go down my list. "We saw each other in college, too, almost by accident. You were visiting friends. We went out that night. Remember?"

Judi nods.

"You held me when my father died," I add.

She looks for her car; we both know where it is.

The thought crosses my mind that if her father dies soon, I might hold her again. I look away, ashamed, and then into my bag and see the box of band-aids. We're all bleeding, I want to tell her. Saying it is at the top of my list.

The bus squeals to a stop. Doors hiss open. The old woman grinds her cigarette into the pavement and boards, toting her chair.

"Thief," I call out to her, with satisfaction.

She turns to face me from the top step. "This one's like new," she says from her perch.

I'm struck by how normal she looks. Not mean, or ill. Tender. She reminds me of my grandmother, who lost much of her family in the Holocaust. In America, all of her possessions—no matter how tattered— were *like new* to her, as if a thing's real history was too troubling to consider. Maybe Judi is reminded of her grandmother, too; we're all peas in a pod here. The doors fold closed. The woman and her chair disappear. The bus lurches forward, and as it passes us, broken windows pull its thousand suns along.

The Dissolution of Rebekah Stern

The September sun was hot and the nights warm and the market good, so the pickle harvest continued. The migrant workers had finished for the day and the fields that Rebekah Stern drove past on her way to the church were empty except for the white plastic buckets they had left, scattered like seagulls in hills of faded green and ochre.

Time, defined in Bear County by the harvest and measured in bins and lugs and crates, was crashing down on Rebekah. She had become what she had yearned to be: a state-employed social worker in the Lake Michigan fruit belt. Above all, she had wanted to show the farmworkers that she was an advocate for human rights and the dignity of manual labor. That even though she'd been born into privilege, she understood.

And now this.

Her director was accusing her boyfriend, the crew leader Carlos Dávila, of welfare fraud. Then a reporter for the *Bear County Almanac*, Mark Silver, phoned her this morning inquiring what she knew about unaccounted benefits, as well.

"Rumors," she'd told Silver. She'd heard them before.

"A farmworker approached me outside Hansen's Grocery yesterday," Silver said. "Asked how much cash I'd give him for $500 worth of food stamps. I said, feed your family. He said they were in Texas. The fact is," Silver went on, "a single applicant with no income is eligible for $28 of food stamps. As you know."

"He could've gotten them anywhere," said Rebekah.

"He showed me his certification letter from your department. Five-hundred dollars. Dávila thinks it's odd, too."

"See my director, Mr. Roy," Rebekah said.

"He won't talk to me," said Silver. "And until someone from your department does, my editor says I have nothing."

"Well, there's another fact for you, Mr. Silver," she said coolly, hanging up. Rebekah then dialed Roy's secretary, Gina, said she needed to see him. She took a deep breath. Going to Nelson Roy's office was like entering a crawlspace; you made yourself small. And even if you emerged without spider eggs and insect wings clinging to you, you still felt dirty. He'd ask you out, or call you out. Six feet tall, single, 30-years-old—a few years older than Rebekah—Roy's long blond hair, surfer boy good looks and tailored suits stood out in rural Stillwater, the county seat.

Roy's floor-to-ceiling windows in a corner office overlooked the parking lot and beyond that, the bay. Over his desk hung a portrait of the president, Ronald Reagan. The director told Rebekah to sit. He was not happy she took the reporter's call. (Gina, the gatekeeper to the office, told him everything that went on. She also was said to have one hand in the pot, and the other down Roy's pants.) Roy said that he knew townspeople were talking about a number of migrant workers who were spending freely, and their newfound wealth was attributed to a giveaway at human services. He would not ask central office for help, however. "They don't promote suckers," he said. But he might have a clue to what was going on, and he was asking Rebekah for help. Today.

"A janitor at St. Joseph's Church allegedly found a state computer in their basement," Roy told her. "Maybe one, or one of several, never returned to Lansing in exchange for new Dells that the agency was promised. And never got." He told Rebekah to drive to the church in Crystal Valley, and investigate. Roy would let her take the remainder of the day off, and start her planned trip to visit her family early. "Maybe you'll run into your friend Dávila there," he had added.

***

Was Roy onto something? thought Rebekah, as she passed a truck turning into the cannery some miles from the church. Or maybe the rumors about Gina were true. Rebekah wanted to believe that Carlos had nothing to do with it, despite Roy claiming—from the moment she was hired in April—that the crew boss was hacking into the state's benefits system to divert food stamps and cash assistance to his friends. "Equal access may work on paper," Roy would complain at staff meetings—waving thick policy bulletins from the Feds that demanded parity for migrant farmworkers—"but in practice it means equal access to screwing the system." Locals didn't much work the fields anymore, and the migrant families the farmers hired relied on government benefits to supplement wages dependent on the crops, market and weather.

Rebekah had felt uprooted that spring moving so far north, yet unmoved by her mother's entreaties to return home, downstate. Farm lives and open spaces—as well as the practice of social work—were new to her. She was a city-girl, and the population of Stillwater was less than that of a suburban mall downstate on a Saturday afternoon. Nature to her had been a show on *National Geographic*—and now she was in it. Big, and little things surprised her. A bear was sighted downtown behind the hardware store. Along the Stillwater River, rows of perfectly round and frosted muffin-like chunks of ice bobbed in the current, and her pulse quickened watching them crowd each other like bumper cars in the narrow river channel before swallowed by the open water of the lake. Along country roads, the daffodils pushed through what remained of the snowpack, and the mudded ruts were drying up. Migrant families arrived from South

Texas to harvest the county's rich asparagus crop, and her agency struggled to meet their needs: housing, for those who arrived without a commitment from a farmer; food stamps; medical appointments and hospital services (as non-residents, they were not eligible for Medicaid); and the unending parade of emergency requests. Small cinderblock houses and seasonal trailers were bursting with life again in orchards and fields, and in yards and driveways babies cried, grills smoked and pickup campers were fixed after the long haul north.

From asparagus to cherries to apples the office reeled like the midway at the county fair, as farmworkers—from such places as Harlingen and Wauchula, San Juan and Edinburg—tried their luck at various games, determined to turn the tables and call the chips theirs. Rebekah learned two things that summer: Clients who understood the rules beat the house; and even the most larcenous among them rarely understood the hand they'd been dealt. She was proud of herself for figuring this out, and she was ashamed, too, for her part in a system that turned honorable persons into beggars, and beggars into thieves. *What am I eligible for?* had become, in sickness and health, *What am I entitled to?*

Carlos Dávila thought they were entitled to plenty, and he sparred with Nelson Roy all season. Darkly handsome, his face weathered by sun, wind and road, he was the first to reach out to Rebekah when she moved north. She would defend him among staff against charges of meddling and fraud, knowing full well that Dávila thought computers were an intrusion, merely another means for the establishment to say *no*. By strawberries, they'd become a couple. From Dávila she would learn of droughts and mites, the *Día de la Independencia* and the coming *Día de muertos*. With him she'd go to church weddings, baptisms and festival dances.

But Rebekah's upper-level courses hadn't covered the misuse of state property or illegally diverted funds, she thought as she turned off the two-lane highway this day. From a hill above St. Joseph's, she watched the dust from tractors settle over the road below. She had wanted to tell Roy that she indeed hoped Carlos was there. They hadn't seen each other in four days, and that felt like four days too many. She wanted to tell Carlos that Mr. VanSlyke had agreed to rent her his daughter's old farmhouse, and she didn't plan to live there alone.

Rebekah parked her car in front of the brick and stucco building, it's steeple rising among the silos in this quiet country village, and in the churchyard dew-washed crosses glistened in the morning light. She walked to the side door that led to the church basement. Finding it locked, she knocked, and knocked. Finally unlatched, it creaked open. She shouted out a hello, but all she heard back was something mouse-like scampering away.

A child, she thought. She followed the steep and chipped cement steps down into the cellar, and the chill made her shudder. When her eyes finally adjusted to the dimness, Rebekah saw a dozen or so people scurrying about banquet-like tables, boxing computers and assorted hardware.

She recognized Mr. Gomez, Mrs. Limón, Sarita Madrigal's son, Jesse, Rebekah's neighbors Betty and Jeb, and Juanito, the caseworker she had let go. Some wore fatigues. Carlos emerged from the shadows.

"What the?" said Rebekah, her voice shaking. "I expected to find USDA boxes of milk and butter. Not the Michigan Militia." A small, nervous laugh escaped her lips. "Mr. Roy said a state computer might be here—"

"We sell your old hardware," Dávila said. "Nothing more."

"The unexplained payments and benefits flying out the door, Carlos? What about that?"

"Yes, the farmworkers are very much into hacking," Dávila smiled, and the wrinkles around his eyes that once had appeared to her so worldly and magnetic, so charmingly defiant, now in fact made him look old and corrupt. "Weeds!" he shouted, in a tone that frightened her. "It's hard work, without benefits."

"And those mysterious government checks Roy told me about, clearing some bank in Matamoros?" said Rebekah. "Files missing? Jesus, Carlos, what were you thinking?"

"I have nothing to do with any of that," said Carlos, reaching out to touch her. "The money we get goes to families your director cut off." Now his tenderness had returned. That voice she'd leaned into, that voice she'd needed for selfish reasons—she now realized—as much as anything else.

She remembered their first meeting. How Carlos had talked about the distribution of wealth in the country, and in the same breath, reparations for migrant farmworkers. It was her best vision of the world, the way it was supposed to be, a willingness to walk the talk. The Stillwater River flowed into Lake Michigan and the Rio Grande into the Gulf of Mexico, and this man had a foot in each. Touching him, she could touch *that*, a passion so deep yet transparent that it seemed to roil his skin. He was electric. They had laughed together, drove the county fields and orchards together, and later, slept together. And now this. She was filled with admiration and contempt for him. And the fear, too, of which might prevail.

"We're not robbing banks," Dávila said.

"Maybe not, but there's principles. You're still breaking the law."

"No one says a thing when the farmers get relief after a drought, do they?" Carlos scoffed. "Washington even pays them not to grow crops. Do they pay us not to eat? Principles are what gringos shout when they lose money."

"You are a reckless, selfish fraud!" she railed at him. But Rebekah knew she might as well have been speaking to herself. Trying to fit in. Thinking she was part of the migrant culture, that she wanted what they had, a hardscrabble existence and dirt under her fingernails. She looked at the farmworkers, watching her and Carlos, decent people who toiled in the fields all their lives. She'd been a student most of hers, first dipping graham crackers into warm milk and watching sitcoms with her overweight dog. Then an English major. Grad school.

The chill and dampness of the room no longer made her shudder; Rebekah was, in part, numb. She saw the crease of daylight beneath the door at the top of the stairs. She wanted to run there and into the blistering sun to examine what she had been blind to: her lover's dark business; her own darkness, too. She started up the stairs.

"What will you do?" Carlos asked.

"I haven't decided." Nelson Roy had told her to call as soon as she knew something. "I was on my way to my grandmother's. She's in a nursing home and not doing well. At least, that's what I had planned." She knew, too, that she'd pass the state police post at the edge of town. "Or should I look over my shoulder for the big bad wolf?"

"I would never hurt you."

"You already did."

They stood in the semi-darkness, she one step above him and looking squarely in his eyes. The color of blackened steak, she thought. And still on fire, one that she had been blissfully unwilling to run from. Or unable. Again, she started up the stairs. Carlos put a hand on her shoulder.

"Your grandmother," he said. "She's cared for by strangers?"

"Is your revolution going to fix that, too?"

"My revolution is about truth."

"Then the truth is, it's over."

Brave words, Rebekah thought as she walked out the door, mired in doubt. On the way to her car she stopped at the sign posting the schedule for mass, and read the words in bold below:

The harvest is simply this
Know God or no God
Pick wisely

She had never before turned to the Almighty for help. Maybe it was time. To pick wisely, and come to know God. The God of all things and all people who would help her sort this out. That was what she wanted.

It was a long drive to see her grandmother and mother, Golda, but there was little traffic. A tease of golds and reds streaked the treetops. An hour out, she stopped for gas, called Carlos from the payphone, then hung up on his answering machine. She wasn't sure what she'd say, if he had answered. Mostly she wanted him to acknowledge the position his actions had put her in. Did he expect her to be a cheerleader and camp follower of his scheme until, poco a poco, her heart and career both withered? Until she was let go for conduct "unbecoming of a state employee"? She remembered the oath she had signed in spring. Things were about to bloom then; there was promise. Her mind raced on, the car sped along, and the leaves in the now dwindling woods were no longer turning colors.

Rebeka called Mr. Roy at a rest area outside Lansing. She told the director that she had nothing to do with Dávila and the computers. It was news to her as well. She wasn't even sure whose they were. He wasn't keeping the money, if he was selling them, she said. When she hung up, she wondered if she still had a job, and if not, what she would do. Maybe she could transfer to the Detroit area, as her mother had practically begged her to. She imagined the reference Roy might give her: *a bitch of a hard worker sleeping with a Mexican thug.* She had refused to have drinks with him more than once. Refused to step on his boat. Even so, the need for child welfare workers, her specialty, was high; sadly, it was a robust business.

Merging with traffic on the highway again, Rebekah pictured herself living downstate. She would miss the lake, and jogging past the farms and orchards where she'd see the Mexicans at work. Miss, too, seeing Carlos there, loading the day's bounty onto a flatbed truck, or talking to a farmer. Months ago the distance between Stillwater and suburban Detroit had given Rebekah strength, a newness and vigor. But now this same road seemed more like sand than concrete—suspended, as she was, between two cultures, seduced by one, too familiar with the other—and her footing was uncertain. *You can't ever go home again she though*t, and laughed out loud.

She'd last seen Golda on Mother's Day, and had told her over lunch that she was falling in love. Golda half-smiled. Rebekah wanted that to be the end to her mother saying that she'd never meet anyone up there. As if *up there* was Siberia. She knew the types of men Golda wanted her to date. Professionals, academics. A house in the suburbs and a cottage at the lake. Men who hired others to get their hands dirty. But Rebekah was in it for the long haul; if a man couldn't fix a leaky faucet in the light of day, how would he pin a diaper in the middle of the night? "Who is it?" her mother said, half-smiling. Rebekah said her boyfriend's full name, slowly pronouncing each syllable. *Car-los. Dá-vi-la.* And it worked. Then. End of conversation. She truly was *up there.*

***

A handful of residents and visitors occupied the nursing home lobby, and small children ran about tossing bright coins into the fountain. Rebekah waited at the front desk for the receptionist. "I'm here to see my grandmother, Anna Katz," she said to a heavyset Afro-American woman of about fifty. Her name tag said Rosie.

"Anna darling!" Rosie shouted to a woman seated by the door. "You have a visitor."

Rebekah turned. "Oh! I walked right past her," she said, then hesitated. "When I talked to my mom, she said I was supposed to ask you for a book? A booklet or something."

Rosie handed Rebekah an application for public assistance. Rebekah started to say something, then looked away. Her heart skipped a beat. "Is something wrong?" the receptionist asked.

"No. I don't know," said Rebekah. "I thought my mother meant something else."

"When people say *book* here, they usually mean that. Your mother wants to apply for Medicaid for your grandmother."

"Yes," said Rebekah softly. "Pages six to nine, columns A through H." She knew each page of the application, and each was the story of someone's life—someone else's; the entries were not supposed to be hers. Her family didn't apply for assistance. She was certain there had been a misunderstanding.

"The social worker will be in Monday," said Rosie. "If you or your mother have any questions."

Rebekah went to her grandmother and knelt alongside her. Anna was looking at everything and nothing from the oversized upholstered chair that she seemed a part of, her deeply lined face without expression. She had an inoperable tumor in her liver.

"Hello grandma. It's Rebekah." Then, louder: "Grandma. It's Rebekah. Golda's oldest."

"Rebekah? Are you married?"

"No, grandma."

"They steal from me here. Combs, jewelry."

"We put your jewelry away. My mother has it. Golda."

"*Voo iz Golda? Vaws vawlt eer geh-Valwlt?*"

"*Eekh red nawr* English, Grandma. Please talk in English."

"Forgive me. You went far away to study. To Spain, didn't you? But you don't speak Yiddish. So my Golda is here?"

"No, not today. I'm on my way to see her." Rebekah puzzled over what to say next, and apologized for not visiting earlier. Anna said that she didn't hear so well, and had to put her head in the *telebishen* to see it. She then turned to Rebekah, her moist brown eyes disproportionately large behind the thick lens of her glasses. "How old am I?"

Rebekah chuckled at the childlike innocence of the question. "Do you remember? I wrote a paper on you in college. You were born in Poland the same year *America the Beautiful* was written on a mountain top in Colorado."

"Is it beautiful today?"

"You came to New York when you were 19 and worked in a sweatshop in the garment district. When you had earned enough money, you sent for your brother Sam, then Tante."

"Aunt-Aunt," Anna said, and the two women laughed at the memory. *Tante* was Yiddish for Aunt, and Rebekah had grown up calling her grandmother's younger sister that, *Aunt Tante*.

Anna wiped her lips with the back of her hand and cleared her throat. "Six dollars a week they paid me. I was the best."

"We're all damn immigrants, aren't we grandma?" said Rebekah. The sun streamed through the high windows and for a moment she watched the accidental rainbows that danced along the edge of the large petal-like fountain.

"I don't remember," said Anna, waving a frail hand then pressing herself deeper into the chair until only the oversized curls of her white hair showed, stiff as straw.

Rebekah leaned over her. "*Bubbie*, when you lived with us before you remarried and we shared the same bedroom...do you remember that? You slept so loud! I thought the paint would fall off the walls. I didn't know women snored. I was afraid that you were going to die in your sleep. I was so afraid." Anna raised her head. "I had bad dreams," Rebekah continued. "And then I thought that if you did die, I'd have my room back all to myself." She squeezed the old woman's hands and could not hold back her tears. "I didn't want you to die, Anna. Not then. Not now."

"You were dating a nice boy. Richard. I knew his family."

"That was in high school. I finished graduate school, and I work now."

"Where?"

"In a small town up north. With one stoplight, one grocery and the closest synagogue 40 miles away."

"How many are there?" said Anna.

The question confused Rebekah

"*Nu, iz yidn dortn?*"

"She wants to know if there are any Jews there," said Rosie from the front desk.

Rebekah looked at Rosie, who did not make eye contact. Carlos once said that Mark Silver was Jewish, but she could think of no one else. Now she wondered if Silver would report Davila's business at the church, if he were to find out. She turned to the fountain where the late afternoon sun from the high windows played tricks on the water, making it appear to flow in reverse, which made her stomach uneasy.

The day had become like a dream to her, one that any minute she'd mercifully awake from as a better daughter, and granddaughter. A better employee. A better Jew. Rebekah looked at the application in her hands and wanted to tear it to shreds. She clutched the granola bar in her purse, realizing that she hadn't eaten since leaving her apartment. Already she was longing for the wide-open north, where she could climb the dunes above Lake Michigan barefooted and scream at the top of her lungs at the waves, and God. The Great Lake was the first place she had ever missed the moment she was away from it, and now, visiting Anna, she understood the losses that came with her gains.

The lobby turned quiet; the residents had retreated to their rooms, or the cafeteria. Anna slept in her chair, an afghan pulled to her chin. Rosie told Rebekah there was a call for her, and directed her to a phone stand across the lobby. Rebekah, assuming it was her mother, picked up the phone and turned to where she could still observe Anna.

"Hello."

"Your mother gave me this number," said Nelson Roy calmly. "Carlos Dávila was arrested today. The church basement was like a damn flea market. And all of it from the Department of Human Services." There was a pause. Roy then asked, "Is there something you want to tell me?"

"Selling discarded computer equipment—wherever he obtained it—is not the same as hacking into the system and stealing thousands," said Rebekah. "The man has trouble opening his own email."

"Maybe he had help from someone inside the agency. Someone he's close to," Roy said.

"You go to hell, Nelson," she said. But the line had gone dead.

She rejoined Anna, and sat alongside her.

"Rebekah?"

"Yes, grandma."

"Your Uncle George put himself through law school carrying letters for the government." Anna removed her glasses to wipe them on a dirty napkin she had crumpled in her hand. Rebekah thought that her runny eyes—unmasked, without magnification—seemed to overflow with life, and yet were oddly vacant, too. "Are you well, Golda?" Anna said just then. "You seem bothered."

Rebekah sighed. "I have some tough decisions to make, grandma.

And you frightened me a bit. Sleeping."

"Georgie delivered mail to my shop in Hamtramck," said Anna.

Rebekah edged away to complete the application for assistance. Her hand was unsteady, the writing unlike anything she had ever done. She knew each question, yet oddly struggled to read them, as the words seemed to float above the page. Her heart pounded in her chest as if she had just completed a difficult run. She pretended to see her answers written by someone else, maybe an unemployed friend from grad school—how whimsical, that! Or a client.

Anna asked if she was doing homework. "You don't have to stay any longer, dear," she said.

Rebekah took the application to the front desk and waited. After some minutes, she left it there and rejoined Anna.

"Excuse me?" Rosie announced. Rebekah turned to see her holding the application by a corner. "You'll need to sign it. Page—"

"Page twenty-six," said Rebekah. She signed, swallowed hard and then turned to the fountain where rainbows danced and the colors blurred.

***

The skies were still clear when Rebekah left the nursing home for Golda's, but the roads clogged with traffic and construction. She thought hard how to avoid it. All of it. At the first stoplight she could go north, then west towards Lake Michigan, and north again along the coast to Stillwater. Or she could turn right and take the highway to her mother's West Bloomfield townhouse, some twenty minutes away. But now her car was stopped, her head spinning. She thought too of her grandmother's application, and how she, Rebekah, in a matter of hours had moved from one side of the desk to the other. Stuck in traffic, she thought of what Carlos had said to her the other week. She was passing Lakeshore Acres, where he worked, when she recognized Josefina, a young girl that her agency had approved as a child care assistant. A handful of smaller children followed Josefina in and out of rows of vines, like ducklings. Rebekah parked the state car and confronted the girl's father. Sweat streaked his dusty face, leaving a pattern like war paint.

"We pay Josefina to watch the children at the camp," Rebekah had said to him. "Not in the field." The mechanization dominating the pickle industry statewide had made few inroads into Bear County, where small hands made for easy pickings.

"As you can see, the camp is right there," the father scowled, motioning to a group of well-maintained trailers across the way. Under a makeshift canopy of bedsheets Rebekah saw a rocker, and the slight figure of an old woman moving rhythmically back and forth, like a metronome. A small dog barked from the driveway. Although they were the same height, she sensed the father looking down on her.

"But I see Josefina here, working," Rebekah said. The young girl then skipped back to the trailer with her siblings and cousins in tow. The crew returned to their labor and Rebekah started for her car. All around her, the sound of cucumbers falling into the plastic buckets was like a gentle and mesmerizing rain.

From out of nowhere, Carlos was at her side. "Harassing my crew?" he teased her. The two walked past his tractor and toward shade.

"The field is no place for kids," she said. "The law says—"

"My first great lesson was in the field," he interrupted. "Picking cherries in Oregon. My father and uncles had crossed some invisible line in the orchard, and a white crew demanded all our lugs. They wanted a fight, and for the Mexicans to get thrown out. More work for them! I was ten, and I understood that. Not the oldest, but the only one who spoke English. I apologized for everything! The hot and dry weather, the shortage of ladders, the price of cherries. But we had work the next day. And the day after that."

Who was she, Rebekah now thought, to tell someone else rules and regulations? *Who was she* to chart right from wrong, black from white, ignoring the fucked-up gray in the middle where everyone just did what they could, trying their best not to be torn apart?

North or south? The light changed, and her mother waited.

***

Rebekah approached her mother's door with trepidation, touched the mezuzah on the jamb—more habit, than prayer—and rang the buzzer. When there was no answer, she knocked loudly. The widow Golda, a retired school principal and in good health, was always where she said she'd be. Always prompt. Reliable. When there was still no answer, Rebekah dug into the bottom of her purse, pulled out a key—and laughed out loud. It had been a long time since she last used it, yet the key was there, like Kleenex, or lip gloss, a constant presence in one handbag or another. A relic from *when she belonged,* she thought, a realization that swept her laughter away as quickly as it had come. The key turned easily, and she let herself in. Golda stood in the foyer.

"Mother!" said Rebekah, alarmed. "Why didn't you let me in?"

"I…I really don't know," said Golda.

"I was worried that—"

"I'm sorry. It's such a silly thing," said Golda.

"What is?

"The key. I wanted to hear it turn in the door."

The women hugged, and with her mother's body pressing against her Rebekah realized that Golda, no longer chasing after first graders, had softened. The once angular hips were now rounded, the shoulders thicker, the neck less taut. Still, she was undeniably attractive. "I might have turned around and left," said Rebekah. "How did you know I'd have a key?"

"Because home meant something to you," Golda shrugged, and started towards the kitchen. She wore a designer warm-up suit that complimented long, strawberry blond hair which she had tied back, not a strand out of place. Her living room, too, was immaculate. A picture of a bride and groom—Golda with Rebekah's father—stood on a side table. A black and white portrait of Anna, Golda, Rebekah and her younger sister Judith with her infant son hung on a wall, framed by small and finely decorative mirrors from Golda's travels abroad. Only the baby was unsmiling.

"I heard you laugh," Golda said. Then added, "I don't think you looked for it long. The key, I mean." She offered her daughter some leftovers, and they sat. "You've lost weight. Are you eating?"

"Yes, mother. I've been running."

"Did your grandmother recognize you?"

They talked about how it used to be, and the trip the three of them had made to New York only summers ago. Mother and daughter rarely allowed the other to finish a sentence.

"Your grandmother had such strength. Such resolve," Golda said, stifling a sob. "And she's so proud of you. Did she ask about your work?"

"The less, the better."

"Oh! Did Mr. Roy reach you? He said it was urgent."

"We talked," Rebekah said, staring at her plate.

"I don't know why you went up there. So far away from what you know."

"Caring isn't a matter of geography," said Rebekah.

"I would think there's little opportunity for advancement up north," Golda said. "To have a good career. To meet someone and—"

"You mean someone Jewish!"

"I never know what to say to you," said Golda.

"The receptionist at the Home gave me the application."

"Is that why you're so upset?"

"If you wanted me to pick up a damn application for public assistance, why didn't you just say so! You called it something else all summer, a *pamphlet* or *book*."

"But that's what they told me to ask for! I knew you were more familiar with those sorts of things, and would do a better job completing it."

"You're right, mother. I see these applications every day. Generally, from people who have little. Or nothing."

"Maybe they want to save what's left."

"Mother—Grandma applying for Medicaid! What about her property? We are not a family who applies for welfare!"

"She has nothing."

"Now, but she did!"

"Would you have preferred to go to Wayne State instead of Brandeis? I didn't hear you complain then." Golda started to clear the table. "It's perfectly legal. Your aunt and I converted her assets years ago. For the grandchildren."

"So the government can pay her long-term care."

"So the family isn't left homeless, and you and your cousins have something to start your lives with!" Golda stood at her daughter's side, wringing her hands. "What am I guilty of? That I, a mother of moderate means, love my children and put their needs above the state? Somewhere in that *meshuga* head of yours you know that we care most for what's closest. It's nature's way."

The words struck Rebekah like a punch in the gut; for all her mother's meandering, she cut to the chase with indeliberate and disarming ease. She got to her feet.

"Where are you going?" said Golda.

"To my office. I'm sorry."

"The office?" said Golda. "Your office is across the state. You just got here."

"You made me think of something," Rebekah said. "Something good."

"What did I do so good that inspires you to leave?"

"That we care most for what's closest."

Golda turned away from Rebekah to look out the kitchen window. Her shoulders slumped. "I made your room up. I haven't seen you all summer. The Holy Day starts tomorrow at sundown. Did you forget?"

"I'll call when I get there."

"Is it trouble with Mr. Dav-ilo?"

"Yes. Trouble with Mr. Dávila," said Rebekah. He had never lied to her, and she believed him now. She embraced Golda, then pushed her gently away.

***

Approaching Bear County at sundown, Rebekah saw wisps of black smoke rising, and within a few miles passed an orchard where in the center small piles of brush burned. She thought of her career going up in smoke, as well. What then? Pick apples with Dávila and his crew? She smiled at the thought. She turned her car into a picnic area along the great lake, smooth as glass as far as she could see, then walked down the embankment and rocks to the shore. The sun was easy on her eyes as she watched the last of it slip into the water. After a time, Rebekah climbed back up and walked across the two-lane where at the edge of a field she saw the fat pickles too large to harvest, crimson and orange in the fading light, half-plowed under in the loose soil, and left to rot. *Pick wisely*, she thought.

Merritt Reef and The Big Parade

Cooler by the lake was no longer heard on the evening news, and in the sunbaked hills that ringed Traverse City, the cherries—normally at market by now—clung to the trees like peas. Three months of drought and unprecedented heat had shallowed Grand Traverse Bay, leaving it bathtub warm, warmer in July than the locals could remember, and the fruit had suffered for it. Still, the celebration of the harvest would go on. As would the runner, Merritt Reef.

Residents and tourists flooded downtown this steamy Saturday morning, more to watch the festival parade than the half-marathon. The runners anxiously milled about, or stretched against street signs and parking meters that were not roped or chained to lawn chairs and even sofas that enthusiastic parade-goers had lugged down the night before. Reef blinked at a huge sausage in running shoes, and tried to stay cool.

"A good day to race," said an older man in black knee socks, near him.

"A good day to die," chirped another.

"Forget personal bests," bullhorned a race official above the din. "Today you run to survive."

Reef, age 30 and a strong runner, would take his chances. High school marching bands warmed up and strutted past floats that hummed or belched, fairylands and volcanoes, tree houses and dragons as young festival queens—apple, asparagus, trout and cherry, of course—stood fanning themselves in the beds of pickups or front seats of convertibles. A distant trumpet played with Reef's heart: the notes, in and out of range, were slow, haunting, familiar, forgotten. Something that his father would hum? He wasn't sure. His father loved a good parade. He'd clap and whistle at every float that went by.

The sweet smells of cotton candy and buñuelos (elephant ears) hung in the air as well. Men on stilts juggled rosy bouquets and long steely knives as a young boy shouted from his father's shoulders. Seagulls, whiter than the white sun, skimmed the blue-green surf at the marina. The long, tube-like balloon, dressed as a sausage in running shorts and Nikes, stirred in the slightest of breezes, kite-like, then settled down in the flatbed truck where it was moored.

"Hey, Reef!" shouted Mark Silver, his training partner. "Faster than last year?"

A year ago the cherries were on time and Reef, exhausted from working double shifts at the cannery, had overslept and missed the race. But today would be different. He had turned off his phone and gone to bed early. He dreamt—and it was the same dream most nights the past year—that he outkicked his nearest rival at the finish, took first place in his age bracket and got his picture in the Sunday paper. In this dream, Reef was kissed by the festival queen, and he'd awake feeling the cool trophy in his sweaty palm.

Today, on the thirtieth running of the Cherry Festival Half-Marathon, an event that *Runner's World* had called—as much for the heat as for the poorly marked trail—"a summer rite of passage," Merritt Reef had something to prove. The parade was not going to pass him by.

"See you at the podium," he said to Silver.

The runners, smelling of sunscreen and sweat, edged closer to the starting line. Reef took a deep breath. The hot heavy air did not yet singe his lungs.

"One minute," bellowed the starter.

Reef eyed the competition left and right: All perched as one, a wild and frantic knot of anticipation strung together by nerves, will and hope; the same hands-on-watches lean, the slow and the fast, practiced and new, young and old; the same hunger to do well. The man in black knee socks wished him luck. Reef smiled, retied his laces and then turned to face the Jack-in-the-packs behind him, the jog trotters and expansive women in spandex he trained so desperately to stay ahead of.

The countdown started and the chorus of onlookers shouted words of encouragement over the staccato-like drills of the parade's "Briefcase Brigade," the Wall Street pretenders strutting down Main Street.

Waiting for the gun Reef again heard horns, a tuba even, and the same broken melody, slow and familiar. Time stood still, although he nevertheless heard it counted.

And—bang! A thread was pulled, the knot unraveled, the horses let loose from the barn. A flurry of arms and legs stampeded past Reef.

Easy now, he told himself. Only children, dogs and fools sprinted the first mile of a long race. They'd "come back"—or get lost in the woods, Reef chuckled to himself as the mass of runners, like a centipede six blocks long, turned toward the shore.

Easy, now. His each foot strike, like some race day mantra, tapped the familiar words. Don't go out too hard. Easy, now.

Relaxed and cheerful, he watched sailboats leave the harbor toward an endlessly blue horizon. "Six minutes ten seconds," came the split at mile one. *Too fast*, thought Reef. *Easy, now.*

At three miles the lead pack, which Reef was a part of, climbed above downtown as the long string of runners trailed in pursuit. Overcome by heat, a few left the marked route, stepped over a guardrail and scampered down the embankment to plunge pell-mell into the bay. *Quitters*, thought Reef. As he followed the turn and crested the hill he saw the Ferris wheel and the sun's glare on the painted capsules of other amusements that catapulted riders into space. Far past the Midway, a red construction crane was suspended above the hospital and beyond that the forest marked the horizon with a dark and uneven line. Reef knew it was there where the race would be won, or lost.

"Do you believe it?" said Mark Silver, now at Reef's side. He pointed to what looked like a missile darting across the bay.

Reef tried to make sense of it. "The balloon-like sausage tied to the truck?"

"Not anymore."

Eager to explore new markets, farmers were promoting a cherry flavored sausage in the parade.

"Fast food for sure," said Reef. "Let's hope for a happy landing."

"An argument to run under control," said Silver as he surged ahead, his mop of dark hair flapping with each foot strike.

"You know I'm going to medal," Reef said, shaking off early fatigue to match the reed-like Silver stride for stride. "Maybe even take yours, old man."

The two friends often bantered like that on their runs in the hills of Bear County, emitting small talk, like sonar, to gauge the other's strength. Now Silver, older by some ten years, laughed. "At what price? Running 100-mile weeks?" Silver grabbed a water in stride at the five-mile aid station. "I know you," he said to Reef. "I know that you run to work. And work to run." He drained the cup and discarded it. "And that you probably run in your dreams, too." He found Reef's hand and briefly squeezed it before letting go. "I know that when you, Merritt Reef, imagine what you can least live without—sweat is the last to go."

"What are you saying?"

"Life is more than a personal best."

"Maybe so," said Reef. He thought of their last run together, a Friday in June when his shift ended, their footsteps almost imperceptible on the soft dirt trail as they looped back to Silver's farm. Moonlight had settled over the pasture like chalk dust and the song of whip-poor-wills rose from all corners. The evening filled Reef with joy and purpose.

Silver, who reported on local government affairs including farm labor, made Reef feel less self-conscious about working at the cannery where his world followed a seasonal axis of asparagus, strawberries, cherries, peas (which they processed for Gerber's), squash and apples. Whatever crop came down the line, and whatever money he could raise himself for the three R's: rent, running shoes and race fees. "Merritt the Carrot," others teased him at work. The elements had weathered him as surely as if he had gone to sea: a bone deep tan, sun bleached hair (sometimes white) and, as if deep-fried, eyebrows the color of orange peels. The older Hispanic women rolled their eyes when at shift's end he hit the ground running, and the younger ones smiled as he darted past. They laughed at him in two languages and went home to large families in small trailers scattered in the orchards.

Though Reef lived alone, the hour (or three) he ran daily felt, and bewilderingly so, like the only one that was his. Running gave him that: time, paradoxically, to stop and think. Time to celebrate the flesh, a body so finely tuned it would endure great hardship and call it pleasure; time enough—and the longer the distance, the clearer the view—to see also what he had left behind: his accounting degree. And his father, who had paid for it.

Now as Reef tucked in behind Silver at the eight-mile mark of the race, he thought—the way random thoughts come on the move, though they are hardly random—that a long run wasn't unlike his relationship with his father. Each pushed him places he was reluctant to go. He wondered how it was that he could run almost any distance, yet lacked the will to pick up the phone and call home. His father wasn't doing well and Reef had put off seeing him. Maybe he'd go after the race, he told himself. He'd go after cherries, that was it. It would be a short crop, maybe last a week or so. They could settle their differences then. A bushel full of hurt.

The two were as different as a father and son could be. Merritt Sr., an affable plumber from Grand Rapids, humming and whistling his way through life. And Reef, running with blinders on. Nothing about his father even fit, thought Reef. Broad shoulders and bandy legs. The oversized head, as round and bald as a cue ball. That small, tight mouth able to swallow whole giving praise before it escaped his lips. Delicate hands. The absurd nickname: *Ritty*.

Reef was taller than his father, too, and it had always seemed so. In middle school classmates called him *Jack* or *Beanstalk* so he turned inward, away from the jitter of nervous adulation and freakish slurs. There was one voice, however, that he couldn't turn away, and it rang clear as a bell. *Run far*, it said. *Run often*. He followed that call. There would be sightings of Reef all over the city. He ran to school and to his father's shop, to the library or dentist and on errands for his mother. Sweat became his life's blood; a day without running was a day consigned to shadows. At night in bed he continued the dance and his legs twitched, urging him on.

The markers Reef passed, however, were never as clear or better or more pure as the ones just ahead. And that puzzled him, too, to be so satisfyingly content in one breath and yet feel so deficient with the next. Not always, but enough to give him pause. Still, the motion and repetition of running allowed him to sort the music from the dissonance. That was his song: a road, and the will to follow it.

***

"Seventy-one minutes!" shouted the timekeeper at the ten-mile mark. Reef grimaced.

***

Fall, the previous year. From the orchard behind Reef's house the festive cries of apple workers pierced the damp air, and standing on his porch, Reef heard a whistling, too, as Ritty's pickup came up the long driveway. It was a simple tune that Reef had forgotten the words to—Ritty had made up his own lyrics—but he and his sister had laughed plenty at them when they were kids. Now Ritty brought with him a new hot water tank. He turned off the truck's engine and without any other words but "Hello, son," pulled himself up into the bed of the truck and sliced open the carton with a razor-sharp pocketknife, it's familiar black casing worn smooth as a pebble. Everything about Ritty, Reef thought, seemed worn. Still, his father bore his share of the tank's weight as the two men came up the porch stairs and into the kitchen. Ritty squared his shoulders at the door to the basement to align the load.

Ritty hummed while he worked as his son handed the tools over. Reef thought of the other jobs he had helped his father on, and how he had once sawed a hole in the wrong spot in the subfloor of a new house, not even close to where he was told to cut it. His father wasn't angry. "Don't sweat the small stuff," Ritty had laughed. "Make it right, and it's the same stinking shit." He fixed the hole like magic, hands working deftly to smooth things over. A part of Reef never forgot that moment, never forgot the desire to be at his father's side. To not sweat the small stuff. To return to the shop together, wrapped in that familiar smell of cigar smoke and machine oil. The smell of confidence, and love.

Now in the dank air of Reef's basement his father's torch flickered. Ritty bent over to cough and dropped a wrench. It clanked off a pipe, and Reef shuddered.

When they finished his father said, "You probably want to go for a run."

"No," Reef said. "I ran this morning."

"Give it another ten minutes and you can shower," said Ritty, scrubbing his hands at the kitchen sink in cold, sudsy water. "It's a good model. I picked it up at the warehouse yesterday. Your landlady will be pleased." A widowed schoolteacher in Manistee, she had told Reef she'd waive two month's rent if he replaced the old and failing tank. Now he tried to pay his father. "Don't bother with that," said Ritty. Turning to go, he added, "You can't find anything better than canning peas?"

"If richer meant faster," Reef said, "I'd be all for it."

"I did whatever I could for you to be something," said his father, a hand on the door.

Reef stood his ground. "I'm a runner."

"What does that even mean? A runner."

Reef's pulse quickened and his thoughts raced to the trails above Lake Michigan. To abandoned farms and hidden streams, to the scent of apple blossoms in May and the marsh at dusk where the trill of spring peepers had made him want to cry out over the mellifluous din that crowded his every heartbeat. To solitary winter mornings when he was the first to blaze a trail in the fresh snow that had blanketed his quiet village overnight. *Out the door is an open sea*, he wanted to scream at his father. *And every day I fish my limit.*

"I'm not good enough," he said. "Is that it?"

A gentle rain was falling outside and the kitchen windows had fogged up. Ritty stood in his ragged blue parka, his hand, as smooth and bright as porcelain, resting on the doorknob. Fine red lines, trellis-like, seemed to hold back a sadness and discontent in his flecked brown eyes; a weariness that begged to be redeemed.

"What would you have me say?"

Reef wanted to hear him say that he missed, and loved his boy.

"I don't care," said Reef. "Forget it."

***

Reef picked up the pace and reeled Silver in as the trail corkscrewed up the side of a hill and into the shade. "Hey! Don't go getting lost," Silver said. "You'll miss the awards."

"I don't mind the woods," said Reef. "It cools you some."

"Maybe too much," said Silver.

They each grabbed a water from the aid stand at a clearing but Reef's mostly spilled. "Come on!" shouted Silver. "Let's go!" Pass someone uphill, Reef knew, and you never had to look back. The edge was mental toughness. Not to let anyone as good as you prove they were better. Silver took off, Reef in tow. No one followed. But then Silver found yet another gear and pulled away. Or Reef had slowed. He wasn't sure. He struggled to maintain pace on the soft terrain. He had counted the miles, but failed to consider the toll that his fast early splits would later exact. He regretted the water stops he skipped. He regretted a lot of things.

His thighs felt made of glass. With each painful landing, something more seemed to shatter and with it, his world. He hated this race. The bay. Cherries. Silver, too, whose bright racing singlet Reef thought he saw ahead—or was it a whitetail deer that flagged across the trail? Just then and without one word, the older man in black knee socks passed Reef as if he were a mere ghost, marching in place. He hated him as well. The trail markers were fewer now.

Reef sat down on the felled trunk of a large beech tree, and the smooth bark cooled his throbbing hamstrings. This was new ground; he had never once stopped or walked in a race before, much less sat. Not knowing what else to do, however, he got back on his feet. Where he last ran with Silver he encountered a thicket of sumac, the red berries pale and drooping. He listened for other runners, but the woods were still as if the heat had choked the life from them. Not even a fly buzzed. The small clearing and the stand of water cups had vanished, too. He couldn't find the trail, and the trees seemed to close around him. Once on pace to a personal best and age group medal, Reef now shuffled about aimlessly, dehydrated and lost. The air burned yet the forest darkened as he pawed his way through it, searching for a way out.

For a deep, lost moment he saw himself shopping in a forgotten city after-hours. The reflection of an ordinary man in the cold and empty storefront windows at first reassured him: he was not a ghost. He lived. He went to try a door. It was locked tight, not even a rattle. He tried another, and on it hung a sign, "Everything Must Go." The uneven lettering was like that of a schoolboy's. And not until this door, too, failed to open did Reef let go of the tree branch that he was clinging to and remember that he was in the woods above the bay and thirsty as hell.

He then stumbled onto a tunnel-like path thick with pine needles where the old growth had merged around and above him. Far away a light flickered. Daylight he thought, and he pushed himself towards it, over roots, through the tangle and deadfall. And though the light, a beacon to him, didn't appear closer, without reason Reef filled with the vague and feverish sense that he was richer for the chase. Finally, through an opening in the dense cover he saw more fully the shaft of light, a reflection off the crane that towered above the hospital below. He moved in that direction, through the dry high grass and thistle and down a narrow deer path etched into the hillside above a small parking lot. He placed one drunken foot in front of the other. In its essence, running was just a controlled fall, didn't George Sheehan say that? The trick now, he told himself, was to fall forward.

Pavement felt good after the uncertainty of the woods. Reef

watched, mesmerized, as wisps of steam curled and rose from his racing flats. Inexplicably something grazed his head. He swatted at it blindly, as if to ward off a mosquito, then looked up to see the parade balloon with the oversized Nikes dangling in front of him. The sausage plummeted and Reef tripped over its spindly legs. It now lay on top of him, heavier than he could ever imagine, brushing his lips, sticking to his wet skin.

"You fucking clown!" Reef screamed at the sausage. "Get off!"

A car door shut. From the pavement where he lie beneath the balloon Reef watched a young woman huffing two small children past him toward the hospital.

"Don't look!" the woman barked at the boy and girl. "In the parking lot!" she sneered at Reef. "Take your *friend* here and crawl back into to the woods or I'll call the police." She raised her cell phone above her head as if to strike him with it.

Reef thought that crawling might be a good thing, and wished he had thought of it sooner. Instead he got to his feet, grabbed the inflatable by the neck, and in one furious blow of almost all that was left of his strength he struck the balloon squarely in the gut. He watched it sail away, kicking its legs to what looked like a Mexican hat dance.

Reef tried to establish a rhythm. *Easy now,* he repeated again and again, but his feet just didn't get it. They more or less slapped the ground, like fish out of water. He found a side door to the hospital open. The drinking fountain was past the emergency room entrance where, displaced by the new construction, a few beds lined the wall. Reef leaned hard with both hands on the cool steel as he bent over to drink.

"Son, is that you?"

Reef waited, head down, drinking deeply, for someone to answer. When no one did he glanced over to see his father clear as day sitting up in a hospital bed. In disbelief Reef stepped closer and strained to see the name fastened to the patient's wrist, just as the older man folded his thick arms.

"Merritt, you look like hell. What happened?"

The two stared at each other. "A long run, dad," Reef finally said. "And you? What are you doing here? Did your doctor—"

"Doesn't matter much," he laughed. "Same stinking shit."

"Is anyone with you?"

"I'm good. Got a nice view of the bay here."

Reef looked around. The bed was crammed into a dim corridor and there were no windows in sight.

"You in the parade, son?"

"Not this one," said Reef.

"Too bad," said the old man. "You know I like a good parade."

"Can we talk after the race?" Reef said. "I'd better go. I have some catching up to do."

"We both do," said his father. "We both do." He started coughing, and put his hand in the air as if for Reef to wait. "Son?" he said after a minute.

"What?"

"Did you fish your limit out there today?" Ritty's hand, still overhead, turned into a fist and shook with a genuine enthusiasm. The inside of the hospital was a good twenty degrees cooler than the street, and Reef started to shake. "Merritt?"

"Yes?" Reef was halfway to the exit.

"Go easy now, son."

***

You never know, thought Reef as he reentered the half-marathon not far from the hospital's main entrance. *You hear one thing, then another. Maybe his doctor's here now. I'll talk to them both after the race.* He grabbed a water at the 12-mile mark to soak his throbbing head.

He thought he saw Mark Silver ahead. With an adrenaline-fueled surge of joy, he reached out to him. And yet—with his hand on his fellow runner's shoulder—instead anger erupted. "It isn't sweat that you can least live without," Reef screamed. "It's love! It's love!"

The runner (and several others) turned around, puzzled.

"I'm sorry," muttered Reef. "I thought you were my friend."

Reef tailed the last of the runners towards the finish as they dodged festivalgoers darting here and there to watch the parade. Latecomers tugged on their children's hands as vendors hawked cups brimming with cherries from Washington. Reef found himself in the midst of the "Briefcase Brigade," the dozen or so men dressed alike in dark suits who parodied corporate life. They marched in tight circles as fast as he could run and up close he saw that their suits were threadbare, their breast pocket handkerchiefs stained, expensive leather shoes old and worn. He felt beaten down and wanted to cry.

Music exploded from all sides now as marching bands converged on Main Street. Reef separated himself from the brigade and the briefcases clicked endlessly behind him, like the shutters of a thousand cameras. He caught up to a large woman, her racing bib reduced to postage stamp size by her massive frame. He had no strength left to pass her. Two young boys in the crowd along the curb jumped up and down on fresh legs, and shouted to the woman. "Mom! You're ahead of Merritt the Carrot! Mom! Merritt the Carrot!"

The woman turned to see what the fuss was about and Reef

recognized Trudy from the cannery. "Hello, love," she said warmly. "You can do it."

Trudy's heart was as big as she was wide. She called everyone "love," and said she was raised in England but someone at work told Reef that Trudy had never once left Bear County. She wore black Capri tights with lime green stripes and a large sweatshirt to cover her girth. Still, she appeared much less fatigued than Merritt Reef. Even her long dark hair remained perfectly braided.

"I know you hurt, love," she said to him. "But you can do it."

Her boys cheered, "Go, Mom, go!" They jumped up and down, buzz cuts pogoing above the sea of faces curbside.

Reef saw Mark Silver past the finish line standing alongside a race official, clutching his medal in one hand and phone in the other. They were looking his way. Reef moved, or was moved, surrounded yet lost—a speck of dust in a pool of molasses—and suddenly he was at ease, out of his body, soaring above the masses and music. Town spread out like a set of toys beneath him. He saw the band shell, and empty park benches. Lifeguards. He saw friends and family. Strangers with love in their hearts. Balloons.

He couldn't tell whether he was floating towards the finish or merely higher, and he wasn't sure it mattered. His thoughts spiraled into a yin and yang. The sky, and bay. Life and death. War and peace. Time, immeasurable. The ticking of a clock from somewhere deep. His journey seemed boundless and he felt remarkably whole, as if he were witnessing a glorious sunset to a perfect day.

The ground slammed into him hard. His ears popped like cap guns. *Bang. Bang.*

Trudy looked at him, smiling, moving as steadily as a tank.

Now Reef heard horns playing the familiar melody, the one that had haunted him at the start of the race. Yes, his father would sing it when he went with him mornings to the wholesaler to pick up supplies. Yes, that was it. That goddamn stupid song. *The Farmer in the Dell*! Only Ritty had changed the words. *The Plumber in the Well*, he would sing. *The plumber takes a son/The son takes a run/Hi-ho, the derry-o/The plumber takes a son.* Reef's legs would not much move, but his heart soared.

"Come on now, love," Trudy said at Reef's side. "We're almost there." Reef stumbled but she caught him by the hand and raised it triumphantly as the two crossed under the finish banner. He held on tight.

***

"Merritt, I'm...sorry," said Mark Silver, helping the spent Reef to his feet.

"For what? I got disoriented. I hit the wall and flipped out. Hugging a fucking tree." He grabbed a cup of sweet cherries from the refreshments offered runners. "I remember shopping! For what, goddamn it? New shoes? A way out? And then Trudy—Trudy!"

"No, no...your sister. She's been trying to reach you," said Silver, his voice cracking. "I'm so sorry." Tears rolled down his sweat-caked face. "Your father..." Silver could not finish the sentence. A white Cutlass convertible turned the corner inches from them, and in the back seat alongside the festival queen from Kalkaska perched a trout ten feet tall with rainbow scales that looked impossibly wet.

"They tried to find you on the course," Silver said. "They even paged you, here at the finish."

Reef started to walk away.

"Merritt. Where are you going?"

"The hospital. I saw him there."

"No, you don't understand," said Silver, catching up to Reef and blocking his path. "Your sister is home. Your father died there. In Grand Rapids. Earlier this morning."

"Grand Rapids."

Silver nodded. "They took him to emergency. She couldn't reach you."

Reef turned to look at the sailboats across the bay. The music started to fade and the hot air pushed down on him so that he was unable to breathe or talk. But still his heart went on, crazily, then slowly, and in that void between the beats was a gap wide enough for the parade to start and the parade to end. *Grand Rapids? But I saw him. Things don't matter much, he said.* Reef was scared and frozen, his wet singlet sticking to him like paste. Silver put an arm around Reef and steered him toward the car.

***

Following M-22 along the coast on their drive home to Bear County, the two friends tried to make sense of the day. "I saw him," Reef said.

"You hit the wall," said Silver. "You saw a lot of things."

"Enough to get back in the race," Reef shot back. "He never had much to say. At the hospital, it was different. He encouraged me."

They drove on in silence, each lost in his own thoughts. Crossing the Stillwater River, Reef looked down to see only a trickle. The summer before, the water was over the road. "It hurts," he said at last. "Like a thousand walls." He looked at Silver, and tried to smile. "Maybe you should write a story about it."

"Merritt Reef and the Big Parade," said Silver. The two chuckled, the uneasy laugh of sadness. "My father sang, more than he talked," Silver said, after a time. "Ritty hummed and whistled, you told me. Maybe they never got the tune right. Or maybe they did, and we didn't hear it."

Easy now, Reef told himself. *Easy now.*

Toxic

The young woman in the tight blouse came out of the landfill office this warm June day and tapped on the van window. Mark had closed it because already the smell was bad. She leaned into the cab. The girls in back tittered. "Stay right," the woman said. "If you go straight you'll end up in a heap of trouble." She smiled, looked to the back seats and said, "You kids let me know if you have any questions." She handed Mark her business card. "You, too," she said. "Anytime."

"The Dutch throw out more than four-hundred thousand loaves of bread a day," announced William, one of two boys in the van.

"Remember," the woman said before waving them on. "Do not go straight."

Mark did not have to be told twice. Married at the age of 40, a father at 50 and divorced at 60, he was good at shunning the straight and narrow; round numbers all, but an uneven path. Today he was chaperoning a fourth-grade field trip to the landfill because, as his ex-wife Ruth had told him last night, *it was his turn*. That is what their lives had become; turns. Now Mark drove the van through the open steel gates, charged up the hill and took the road to the right.

"How come Ruth didn't take us," asked his daughter, Joelle. She was sitting directly behind him and next to her best friend, Philomena. Joelle had started to call her mother by her first name when she and Ruth moved out. As if to say, I want equal footing on ground that was increasingly shaky. As if to say, *let's all be adults here.*

Mark looked at the two girls in the rear-view mirror and wondered if they should have mascara on. Philomena had slept over the night before, Joelle's first sleepover at his new house. They giggled into the night long after he had told them to brush their teeth and go to bed. In the morning the three of them swung by the school to pick up the boys. One never said a word. The other, William, recited from the report his group was to give later that week. The girls ignored them both. At noon they were to meet up for a picnic lunch with the entire class at a nearby park, then tour the recycling center in a building adjacent to the landfill.

"Americans throw away 5.7 million tons of carpet a year," William said now as the van crested the hill.

"It's just garbage," said Philomena. "Do we have to get out?"

"Yes," said Mark, opening the van doors. "That is what we've come here to do. Look at our garbage."

"Why?" said Joelle.

"An education," said Mark.

"Whose?" said Joelle.

"Americans throw away 28 billion pounds of food a year," said William, taking out a notebook and pen from his backpack.

"Thank you, William," said Mark.

Tossed by the wind, garbage of all types—plastic, paper, soiled cloth and flattened cans—danced about them in small and private eddies.

Mark and the kids joined the half of Joelle's class that had assembled near the edge of a giant crater. The others were visiting the recycling plant first. A bulldozer and two front loaders moved piles of garbage in the pit below. The ground shook and the stink of diesel added to the rot of everything.

"My eyes burn," said Philomena.

From the ridge where they stood Mark could see the southern tip of Lake Leelanau, and the treed neighborhood where he and Ruth had lived and where Joelle was conceived. Where in the past year she lost two grandmothers, one fish and a bird. Life went on; the garbage truck came and the garbage truck left. Until they lost the house, too. These days he didn't have much trash. Mostly it was sorting out what was left.

Looking across the shallows of the blue green lake, Mark thought of it, too, filling with garbage, garbage as bright and bold as lava and as dark as night that no one could stop and still these fourth graders would get on with their lives, making small changes here and there, leaving greater footprints yet here and there, then soon enough boarding buses and planes and going away to school and fighting wars in boardrooms and overseas and how deep must the hole be to contain the blood of all that?

Mark picked up the loose papers that had wrapped themselves around his ankles. Disposing of them seemed the least he could do. When he glanced at the topmost sheet, he stopped dead in his tracks. Philomena walked right into him. "Sorry!" she said. He held a letter from Ruth in his shaking hand, uncertain if his vision was playing tricks on him. The letter was horribly stained and torn, but otherwise intact, and he read it to himself.

> *Dear Mark*
> *You know damn well that the money your mother left you*
> *was intended for me as well. But you had to go to court and*
> *we both lost. Your attorney beat up on me. Mine beat*
> *up on you. Assholes both and the two of us became nothing*
> *more than collateral damage. Despite what those vultures of*
> *bitter endings have done to our family, I want...*

The rest, a few sentences more, was not legible. None of it had he seen before.

"I don't want to be here, Daddy. It's stupid. Everything's stupid," said Joelle.

"I think so, too," said Mark.

"By the year 2050 all the plastic floating in the ocean will outweigh the fish," said William.

"Who cares," said Joelle. And then, to Mark: "What were you reading?"

"Household refuse."

"Is Ruth going to pick us up?"

"Later. At school."

"Can I live with Philomena?"

Mark smiled at her, crumpled up the letter and walked to the edge of the pit where he pitched all the papers that he was holding onto. As they spiraled downward in the wind he wondered, when all was said and done, who would fill the hole that was left.

The Unraveling

When I was married, I wore clothes too large. Pants, jackets, sweaters draped my thin frame like a tarp thrown over a pile of sticks. I felt protected. My ex-wife Ruth said it was because I was trying to be bigger. Maybe better. But isn't that what marriage vows are? A promise to be someone you're not? Fittingly, when the marriage ended, I started buying clothes that were more appropriate. I wear normal sizes now, that is, large, and not extra-large or, in my grandest illusions then, XXL.

Now my friends say that I look too skinny. That I don't measure up. That just maybe I'm not the man I used to be. (Who is? I shot back.) My mother, too, before she died, admonished me for not taking on more. Classical music, ballet. Aeronautics. Cheeseburgers.

I don't want to be fat, or thin. Just whole.

Tonight was my daughter Joey's high school graduation party. She had attended a private school and Ruth and I wanted to do it right. We rented the lavish banquet hall at the country club I no longer belong to. Open bar. Dinner. Five-piece band. For the occasion I bought a stylish Armani-like suit on sale that fit me to a "T." The saleswoman at Macy's had assured me that it wasn't too tight. That is the look now, she said.

My date Angie, a friend of a friend's friend, wore something you'd see on the red carpet in Hollywood, not in a town like ours. She turned heads, is what I'm saying. There was a lot to see.

My daughter rolled her eyes when I introduced her to Angie.

Past the bar on a table were photos of Joey, from diapers to diploma, which I showed to Angie. I was in a few myself. She asked if I'd lost weight. I told her that I used to wear clothes that were too big, trying to live up to what I was not. She turned to the bartender, ordered a martini and said, how sad.

I excused myself and went to the men's room, where things truly started to unravel. There was a row of tall urinals on each side of me, polished, stately, like sailors in dress whites standing at attention. You feel worthy in front of these things; they invite you in close. Too close, alas. Attending to my business, I looked down to find my new Italian calfskin wingtips wet with splash. I cursed, furious, and then was bewildered at my fury. Why should a few drops of pee at my feet burn in my gut, like acid? What absurd standard am I so desperately trying to live up to? I didn't piss my pants. I finished up, finished with staring at the marble wall, then took a cloth hand towel—no paper here—and bent over to dry my shoes.

"Polishing your new brogues?" A voice boomed from a ways down.

I straightened up. It was Herb, my ex's fiancé. A stockbroker with a body so chiseled he looked like a small truck doing a wheelie, the underbody like glazed acrylic. He wore a flattop, too, flat enough to serve drinks on without spilling a drop. He said I was looking fit. I said yes, hello and thank you. I never liked him much, not because he was dating Ruth, but rather…he was arrogant, well-built and knew a lot about money. And was dating Ruth. There was the time, too, when Ruth and I were having a spat over child support and I didn't know I was on speaker phone. Until Herb said, "You're bigger than that, Mark."

On our way out of the bathroom, I made certain to open the heavy dungeon-like door for him. It took a good push. When the door closed behind me, it brushed my coat sleeve. I thought nothing of it, and rejoined Angie at the bar.

At our table a short time later, between the serving of the salad and entrée, she started to pinch and tug at my elbow. A signal, I thought. The start of something grand. I pressed my thigh into hers. She smiled, and tugged all the more. My funny bone leapt with joy. My heart soared. But silver threads and golden needles it wasn't going to be. You might say loose ends bothered Angie.

The head of school stood up to speak, and the music stopped. He thanked Ruth and me for the privilege, as he put it, of entrusting to his care Joey's desire for a higher learning. He asked Joey to stand, and she looked lovely in her soft blue crepe gown (half of which I had paid for).

Angie started to tell me something, just as the guests stood and applauded.

As I stood, however, the right sleeve of my suit coat slid from my elbow to rest at my shirt cuff, held by only a robust thread or two. Angie's hand went to her mouth. A minor calamity; few, if anyone, had yet noticed the doughnut-like bangle on my wrist. Rather than applaud and risk exposing my wardrobe malfunction, I raised the fist of my good sleeve overhead to cheer Joey. But guests—some dozen tables—thought I was asking for quiet to make a speech. They sat down. The room was still, or nearly so, as several people squirmed right and left in their chairs to better see me.

Terrified, I looked back at them, these faces plump in their riches, or fearsomely desiccated, staring expectantly at me. What did they see? A dandy and pretender, or candle in the wind? The band started up again. A drumroll.

I simply waved to the guests with my left hand, smiled and started to sit down. Until my well-tailored pants ripped at the seat. Rather loudly. Angie laughed so hard she spit food. From the table next to ours, Herb said, also rather loudly, "probably the blue cheese." More laughter. I turned to see him grinning, and my daughter make a face.

Angie got up and left.

I got back to my feet quickly.

"Please," I begged. "Nothing is what it seems. Nothing." I leaned hard on the table with my hands for support, and emptied my heart. "I'm a thin man," I cried out. "A shell of one, bones and nothing more. This world of ours shelters so much, yet covers so little. I hide from it every chance I get, and dance naked in my dreams." People continued to stare. I looked away, then down at the jumbled threads of my life—family, marriage, daughter, romance—a sleeve now lying like someone's fucking Halloween sock discarded in my empty salad bowl, bits of cheese and shredded carrot stuck to it.

"It's a tight fit, this," I said. "Thank you for coming."

Pictures at an Exhibition

You won't see the picture. It fell out of the box she carried from the house tonight. There's a footprint on it. That should tell you something. Not a picture of a foot. You know what I'm saying. I don't think that she turned around and stomped on it. Walking over it would have been enough for her. She'll say it was an accident. She says that about a lot of things.

You won't see the picture. As I said, it fell out of a box. She still has the others of us. The Tetons. Grand Canyon. Rafting the Upper Klamath. Disneyland. Pictured Rocks. A box load of pictures of when we were younger and laughing and she was the center of my universe. And of all of them, this one falls to the floor. Of when I am not so young. Or happy. Or going anywhere. Maybe this one was the last picture shot. From the happiness to not. In between were the years of *You don't understand me.* And *You don't like my friends.* And *What is it that we have in common?* And on and on. Once, returning home after a night out she said, *You don't know who I am.* I stared at her brown eyes as she squinted at me. Maybe the light was painful for her. Maybe I was. I think she was high.

You get the picture. Did she purposely drop it for me to find? If so, what was the message? That she could move on without my baggage? That there was no room—in a box, no less!—for whatever it was that "I" brought to "us?" Maybe the picture fell when the door opened and a gust of wind took it. And she stepped on it by accident. Maybe that was it.

You won't see the picture. But the one I wished she had left or dropped or given back was of the two of us walking in the rain. It was years ago and I don't know who took it. The streetlamps had come on and the light that reflected up from the little pools of water on the bridge over the Boardman River below made it look more like a painting. A Monet. The street looked like Paris. It wasn't. I never took her there. The picture was taken near our home that she hated in a town that she loathed on our way to dinner at a charming tavern that she despised. I'll go with you this time, she had said. She put her arm around me and looked surprised that the camera was there, that someone wanted to catch the moment. She was young and innocent and still capable then of clawing her way back—when she tried hard—to the reality that I cared deeply for her. She held me tight, tight enough to leave a mark. Maybe she feared slipping into the abyss of hate that would soon swallow her.

Maybe it had been planted by then. A seed that I could not see growing. I asked her that once. Where does all this hate and disdain for others come from? The world is fucked, she said. It doesn't love you back. I'm leaving she said, but didn't. Then.

We went to counseling. Picture that. I looked at the therapist's books, and the photos on the wall. A young boy in a wheelchair. His wife (who I vaguely knew) in an evening gown. His daughter playing soccer. These are the images, he said from over my shoulder, that sustain me. He made us tea and said this: do not ever let the sun set on your anger. I said how does that work? She doesn't come home. She said that I overreact. I said that you are good at running. And not so good at admitting hurt because that would mean that you actually cared.

I think about the other pictures in that box. Of friends we no longer have. Parties we no longer go to. Birthdays we no longer celebrate. Holidays, parades, baseball games.

I'd rather she'd left them in some large hall, a canyon perhaps. Or church basement. A lost and found of unclaimed pictures. And you'd find printed on their backs, like baseball cards, the subject's history in the majors. In life. Who they are, and how they did. You could sort them, the faces and feelings and performances, pick who'd you want on your team and, later on, maybe even trade one for a different card. Someone not a free agent.

There's a car outside. It's been idling for some time. I go to the porch, and she is standing at the curb.

I love you dad, she shouts. I'll clean up the mess later.

Spilled Milk

The snow had stopped, and sunlight streaming through the barren trees cast stark shadows on the snow-covered hills surrounding the two skiers. "She's my sister, for God's sake," Allie said, turning her skis sideways on the trail to face Mark. She withdrew her hands from her mittens and pole straps, unzipped her waistbelt and checked her phone. "They'll be here soon. And I'm going to love my new nephew regardless."

"Too much fucking money," Mark said. Until then his only complaint was icy trails. Now he thought of propelling himself alone into the white and trackless unknown, past the climb to Allie's gate and state land that abutted her property. He wasn't looking forward to meeting her sister Jill and the new baby.

Allie's family, with all their brilliance and millions—on both sides—frightened him. They hired birth mothers and took vacations in the Alps; he was saving up for new skis. Allie's daughter was on the honor roll; his, on probation. The couple had been together for three years, and Mark had lost count of all the times he'd wanted to run. He lived 200 miles north of her West Michigan home, where he was a reporter for a chain of rural newspapers. There was refuge in distance.

Now Mark stabbed his poles hard into the ground, launching himself into the climb to the gate. He did not ascend the hill gracefully. Rage pushed up from his blood, and snow—dislodged from low branches by his flailing ski poles and wild effort up the narrow path—stung his burning face. Attacking the hill only fueled his anger, however; the more he pushed, the more it came. At the child abuse and neglect that he reported on. At his words that were never enough. At state government and underfunded foster care, where only the lucky kids got out. At the sister, and her designer baby.

Allie caught up to him outside the house. "Why didn't you wait—"

"Why didn't she adopt? Your purse-proud sister is fifty-something and already has a family."

"Kids from foster families are older, and many of them damaged," said Allie, cautiously stepping out of her skis. "You know that. Jill was lonely and wanted another child of her own."

"Her own?" Mark sneered.

"Then discuss it," said Allie. "Don't run."

What more was there to say? The divorced Jill had an adult son, two children in college and a daughter in high school living at home. She was coming from Boston. Mark gathered their skis and stormed off to the garage, rage eating at him like piss through snow as every gripe he had about Allie boiled over. Her snail's pace. Bluntness. Eidetic memory that recalled, scene-by-scene, their past disagreements and where she thought he had screwed up. At times their every difference felt like an assault, and could send him packing.

And now, the sister.

Mark hesitated before entering the house. He thought of sitting out the company in one of the empty bedrooms upstairs. Or perhaps the cellar. No one ever goes there. Maybe the housekeeper would bring him food; Mark didn't think she liked the idea of Jill's visit, either. He could hide out for days in a house like this. Allie's children were in California with their father, a cardiologist. He, his brothers—one an engineer, the other a salesman—and their father, a physicist and inventor, developed and sold medical devices to Johnson & Johnson. Allie had held onto her stake in the business. And to the house. *Downton Allie*, Mark called it, teasing her.

Now Allie's mutt, Kelev—Hebrew for *dog*—clattered across the hard kitchen floor, glad to see him. The dog would find Mark no matter where he hid, often snatching his trail mix, or underwear, from his pack. Kelev had a nose for trouble.

"I need to go back out," said Mark. "Get some whiskey."

"I don't want to drink," said Allie. "And Jill stopped."

"The milk fairy came and she's breast feeding?"

"Baby Theodore's nanny is a wet nurse. She was also the surrogate, and is with them."

"Is there anything Jill can't buy?" Mark said.

"A wet nurse," Allie said, starting to make lunch, "is a time-honored tradition. Deborah in the Bible—"

"Then why not find Theodore an ass! That worked back then, too."

"Do not be rude to Jill and her baby," Allie said, her voice even, the words measured.

"Disappearing would be an act of kindness," Mark said.

"Selfishness, you mean." Allie was loyal to her sisters, like a dog to a bone. Nothing came between them. Relationships sustained her; he felt strongest alone.

Still, the two had much in common, and at times argued like siblings. Over who got the larger serving of oatmeal. The taller glass of orange juice. And indeed, at *Shabbos* dinner last evening, covering her face with her hands to recite the blessing, Allie reminded him of his mother. She, too, had her own way of doing things: Uncompromisingly.

Sitting on the floor to unlace his ski boots, Mark thought there were few things returned to you in this world—seasons and sunsets, love, if you were lucky. Sadly, your mother was not one of them.

However, Allie was able to do what his mother would not: listen.

"Running is learned," she said, kneeling, a hand on his shoulder, looking into his eyes. "I'm sorry that Jill's choices make you uncomfortable. But I am not my sister's keeper."

Sun lit up the kitchen, spilling, too, off the fresh snow outside the French doors overlooking the trails. Mark sat on a high stool at the counter. Allie sliced open pita bread, which she toasted, and spread tahini on. Everything she did was orderly, methodical. *Sometimes even reasonable,* he told himself. A pediatrician and educator—she mentored Syrian refugee children—Allie had X-ray vision of some kind, Mark was convinced, and the keen light by which she examined all things usually saw through him, too. Into his ire, and shame. That he had disappointed his mother, and not become the *macher* she had wanted him to be. Hadn't made the world a better place. The unease that he hadn't earned the blessings on his plate.

He tried to ward off Allie's probing. Tried everything except a tinfoil hat. But his vulnerability seemed to delight her, and she exhorted him not to hide from (or behind) it. *The Israelites carried two sets of tablets across the desert, she would say. The whole one, along with the shards of what Moses broke in anger. To remind themselves that life is sometime in pieces.*

Now Allie washed and chopped cilantro from the fridge with a precision that marveled him. Her every move was measured, and measured again. Next she was at the stove, roasting almonds. "Some of the family is unsure about the baby, too," she sighed.

"How much does a thing like that even cost?" Mark asked.

"A thing?"

"A surrogate baby."

"More than double your salary," said Allie, turning to face him.

"Did she shop online at some sperm bank and sift through offers of the day like it was Saks? Spend this and get that, delivery included?"

"Why don't you go shovel the walk? Or take Kelev out? They'll be here any minute."

"Too much fucking money," Mark said again, standing. "Forget the drinks. I'm going skiing."

"You said conditions weren't good."

"That I can at least navigate." He kissed her neck, and reached behind her to scoop up some almonds from the pan.

"Don't burn yourself," she said.

He had, slightly.

He went into the garage. Allie lived close enough to Lake Michigan where on a good day—a good day for Mark—enough new snow might fall to at least cover your tracks. Finding your groove in old places, thought Mark, was as pleasant and satisfying as anything.

It was afternoon. The almonds had made him thirsty and he grabbed a beer from the fridge where Allie kept it for him. He felt at peace in the garage. It wasn't as distant as the cellar, but it was large and heated and the beer was cold. He slammed the first one down before the fridge door shut and light went blank. He grabbed a second, then carefully stepped over the widening puddle on the smooth concrete where snow dripped from the skis leaning against the wall.

Now the dog barked from somewhere in the house. A heartbeat later Mark heard a car door shut. The muted cry of an infant. The doorbell. He took a long swig and left the half-empty bottle on the table above the bin of recyclables. He felt a chill and looked down at the floor: his socks were wet. He started to enter the kitchen, shuddered to a stop and sat on the garage stoop. And he wept, overwhelmed by a sorrow he could not name. *Was it the money?* he thought. He didn't even pay for his own beer.

Allie opened the kitchen door a crack, wide enough for Kelev to squeeze through. She didn't see Mark sitting there. The dog licked his tears from his cheek.

***

It was a long journey into night for Mark, alone with his thoughts and the dog. After a time, the garage was cold and empty to him. He led Kelev to the yard, where gaunt and otherworldly shadows of trees moving across the moonlit snow frightened him, and his heart skipped a beat. He caught his breath, and laughed at himself for feeling like a child lost in the woods. Mark laughed at his rage, too, that had blinded him; he would find his way. He walked to the gate, which had been left open. When Kelev tried to dart through it, Mark said, "No, boy. We're going to stay," and he closed it.

Across the yard an upstairs bedroom shutter banged in the wind, unmoored from the brick wall, and he looked that way. He saw light from the window in the room below, a warm glow in the frozen landscape. He thought maybe Jill wanting another baby was like her playing dolls when she was younger, and guessed that she had been incapable of giving any one of them up. Giving up holding, cuddling, showing love and orchestrating their lives. And he wondered, too, what that might be like to be so attached. Not to plastic, but to sinew and bone. Still, he thought the world didn't need baby Theodore. Then his heart sank at the thought that it probably didn't need himself, either. He trembled, not from the cold, but from the loneliness that he felt.

He reentered the house and the stillness of the darkened kitchen. He strained to hear Allie call his name, the guests stir, the baby cry.

"You must be Mark." The voice startled him.

"Hello, Jill. How was your trip?"

"Allie said that maybe you had left. Or were in the garage. What were you doing there?" She flipped on a light.

"Adding things up. Quieting myself down."

"Are garages good for that?" Younger than Allie, Jill had both the same impish grin and square-jaw seriousness of her sister. Their mother died when the girls were not yet teens, and the lifelong raising—or mentoring—children themselves perhaps helped fill an unthinkable absence.

"Yes," Mark said. "As is tromping around the yard."

"Are you upset that I came?"

"Just wondered why…"

"Why Teddy," Jill finished his sentence. "It's simple. I longed for another child, and I have the means. So why not?"

"I have trouble with that," Mark said, without rancor. "There's plenty of kids wanting. Hordes of them. You have to be dumb and blind not to see that."

"I'm not pretending to fix the world," said Jill. "*You* adopt if you're so keen on it."

The voices from the family room hushed now.

"If I were to parent again," Mark said.

"Allie speaks fondly of you. I thought you'd want to meet my son."

Mark wasn't sure that he did. He felt at odds with Jill's ability to manufacture what or who she wanted. That is how he saw it. Nevertheless, he followed her into the family room.

"You've met?" Allie beamed, cradling her nephew with both hands.

"Yes," Mark said.

"I hope you had a good ski," she said, but with a look that said she knew he hadn't skied at all. "This is Kima." Allie nodded to a young woman next to her. "The surrogate, and nanny. Now meet Teddy." She handed up the squirming baby in his white cloth diaper, skin as bright as snow. He settled down at Mark's touch, nuzzling his neck. Mark laughed out loud. What had Teddy done wrong? He was born, and he lived. Nothing more. There was a weightlessness in Mark's arms that felt right and complete and as satisfying as if he had carved a perfect turn in fresh powder, the weight against his skis the same resistance as Teddy's, an irresistible lightness of being.

Mark fell hard that day and held Teddy into the night as much as possible, exploring together the house's quiet places and empty rooms.

Two Candles

It's the second night of Hanukkah and I'm waiting for my teen-aged daughter, Joey. Did she run out of gas? Heard that one. Phone dead? That, too. I straighten the candles on the menorah that sits on a table of my mother's in my living room, and lower the front blind. It's long past sunset. I stick a log on the fire, a CD in the changer, old songs, and listen to *Oh Hanukkah, Oh Hanukkah:*

And while we are playing
The candles are burning low
One for each night, they shed a sweet light
To remind us of days long ago

Days long ago stopped interesting Joey, and I struggle with what she needs from me.

She bursts through the door. The roads were bad, she says. She takes off her boots, leaves her coat in her old room. A hug. She says they—the boyfriend she moved in with—had to drive to Grand Rapids, a three-hour ride in the snow. I don't want to ask what for, but nevertheless am about to when she blurts, "I thought I was pregnant, Daddy." All at once I fill with rage and self-recrimination. *Happy Hanukkah to you, too,* I think.

She says she went to a Planned Parenthood "away from here" because her mother is a health care provider where we live, and Joey was worried she'd find out; she still sees her mother's doctor. A home pregnancy test had given her what turned out to be a false positive, and she was scared. I explain HPPA to her, and she says people talk. She complains of protesters who surrounded her car when they left the clinic. I go to the window and open the blind. Christmas decorations glow softly from a house at the dark end of the street. From where I can't see, someone's wheels spin helplessly, the sound is sharp and close like a buzz saw. The whinnying comes and goes but in the sweep of headlights of an approaching car, there is only the falling snow.

"We are the company we keep," I tell her, staring out the window.

"What's that supposed to mean."

"Why did you move in with him?"

"We've been over that."

"We were going to celebrate the holiday," I say, turning to face her.

"I brought you something." She hands me a small package, wrapped with care and tied with strands of blue and silver ribbon. I left her one gift in the kitchen, a book. Once we lived in a large house, had a larger income, and I bought her a present for each night of Hanukkah. Like my parents had, for me.

The music, stuck in an endless loop, plays on and *days long ago* lump in my throat. I think of all the candles I lit for my mother. The times she waited for the light to go on. For me to be a better student. To study law, or medicine. When I moved away, married a non-Jew and became a father, my mother soldiered on to the next worry: would her granddaughter be Jewish enough? She wouldn't know her long, and held onto a flickering hope that Joey's roots would be well nourished.

Joey and I cling to what hasn't washed away. We light candles, and exchange gifts.

What I had wished for—that one morning she'd jump out of bed, huff down the stairs and ask, *which way to synagogue?*—was as likely to happen on its own as if I'd rubbed two sticks of wax together, looking for a spark. I wanted from her what I lacked myself, a willingness to join the congregation. Disaffection, however, seemed more her calling just as it was mine; religion wasn't anything either of us practiced. "What part of me is Jewish?" She once shouted to me and her church-going mother from the top of the monkey bars at the park, staring at her two fists, small and bright as pebbles in the afternoon sun. As if it was something she had been told, and forgot. As if one hand should be black, the other white.

Perhaps there is no more profound loss than the gift, your heritage, you fail to pass on. I wanted to leave Joey with more than a bucketful of doubts.

Now she reaches out to steady my hand with her own as I strike a match to light the *shamash*, the helper candle. Her hand is warm on mine, despite the cold she came in from. "It was a simple examination," she says, "I'll be alright."

"I'm not sure I will," I say. I struggle with her lifestyle. I struggle on moral and religious grounds. And on no ground at all.

Together we hold the *shamash* and light the first two candles, as I recite the blessing. *Blessed are You, Lord our God, King of the universe, who has granted us life, sustained us, and enabled us to reach this occasion.* The thin wicks catch, almost as one; the candles will not stand upright by themselves, and must lean on one another. It's always a mess of a holiday, any holiday, when I'm in charge. The ceramic Noah's ark menorah that I bought when Joey was a toddler has tigers, giraffes, elephants and bears as candleholders. A few years ago I dropped it on the hard kitchen floor, then glued it back together, piece by piece. Two by two. A tusk or paw is missing. Last night, alone, I failed to light a single candle and wonder how many Jewish laws I violated.

Joey knows the story of Hanukkah, *The Festival of Lights*, but I recount it anyway as we sit. A scant reservoir of oil lasting eight days and nights, lighting and sanctifying the Temple recaptured from the Greeks and Syrians. A miracle.

She laughs, then switches off the lamp hanging above the table.

"You used to believe."

"In the tooth fairy, too, Dad."

"The Bible stories I bought when you—"

"That was *before*."

As in, *before* the divorce. *Before* she moved ten times in five years, shuttling from one rental to another. From parent to parent. *Before* the falling out she had with her mother over marijuana, abstinence and—for good measure—the virgin birth. Joey discarded the mixed bag of faith she was born into like yesterday's fashion. Nothing fit. Tide in, tide out.

Exposed, vulnerable. Beautiful. Stupid. And I want her to know she isn't alone.

"I was 19."

"What?"

"Her name was Kristen and a friend drove her from Michigan to New York, where abortions were legal."

"You never told me this."

"Why would I?" I look away. "I thought of it like a tonsillectomy. Let someone else hold her hand. No one misses their tonsils."

Joey is quiet. "Don't tell my mother," she finally says.

"I could never tell mine."

"Can we not talk about this?" she asks.

So we stare at the candles, now burning low. Neither of us says a word. Animals crouch and leap along the wall. Whatever appendages are missing, they look whole. Vigorous, even. Watching them, I think of the blessing and realize what *enabled us to reach this occasion* must have also, by the law of averages, *disabled us*, too. On occasion. And here we are. It's clear to me this is what I can pass along to Joey: misgivings are as much a link in the chain that joins us as is the rising sun; *the light will stay on*. I feel very clever, and laugh out loud.

"Dad?"

"I was thinking of miracles," I smile at her. "Yours. From diapers to Barbies to blunts in a heartbeat—some 17 years, anyway—making plenty of stupid decisions that didn't kill you. A miracle. Along with stupid decisions made for you. We're each of us dumb, yet alive. Sucking in the same air, breathing out the same despair and unmitigated happiness both. No small miracle that, either."

Joey rolls her eyes. And I think in spite of all the hurt I've done, I've known the love of a brother. Friends. A lover. A daughter. A miracle, that too. That love is always greater than the effort put forth to thwart it.

I think too of all the ways I've failed as a father, a teacher. Did she learn anything?

Still, I want to forgive her. Forgive myself, as well. She's followed no path, for the most part, I hadn't taken first. This shadow, so close to the flame.

The Gingerbread Story

Halfway up Old Mission Peninsula Allie and I left the car in the snowy woods, and looked for the path Luke had plowed to his house. The wind howled over the bay that evening, tried to make us dead in our tracks, and after a misstep or two, we saw his lights. As close to the North Pole as she cared to be, Allie said, shrinking into her long woolen coat. Building a gingerbread house at an office Christmas party is not something Jews generally do, she said, too.

Leaving her house downstate, we had told ourselves it might be fun. A project together. "Putting up walls is something you're good at, Mark," she teased me.

"You're such high maintenance," I said, "it'll never do to construct just one gingerbread house. Where will you summer?"

"Don't forget the chocolate coins!" we reminded each other, laughing.

Still, Allie said that I was throwing her to the wolves. Taking her faraway to party with strangers. Strange traditions. I wanted to go because I loved Luke, my editor, and would follow him to party at sea, if he so wished. Or overboard.

Run as fast as you can, I told her when the invitation came. *You can't outrun me, I'm the Gingerbread Man*. Weary of asking me for support, she didn't laugh. I wasn't there for her when her youngest left for college. Or later that same year when she was grieving again, at the death of her dog. It had been easy for us to go our separate ways, north and south. Distance, she said often enough, that I used to distance her.

Luke met us at the door, joking that the bread crumbs he had left along the path for us to follow were buried under a foot of snow. We shook off the cold and snow, less so the doubts, and after introductions to our hosts and a glass of wine, I thought Allie warmed up to the challenge. All of them. I introduced her to others I knew, and after more wine, to those I didn't.

Following dinner—which included a ham, that we didn't touch—Luke distributed the flat boxes, as heavy as laptops, telling us and the ten other couples invited that it will be a contest: bragging rights, and a bottle of Champagne to the builders of the most imaginative house. Allie and I smiled at each other, as if to say, *We'll construct a house not like any ever seen, and be the toast of the party. We've got this.*

"Chill those glasses," I boasted to the room. "Drinks will be on us."

We couldn't miss, I thought, Allie with her keen interest in architecture, me with a cocksure sense of mechanics and scale. I eagerly ripped open the box and, regrettably, the instructions, too. Out spilled gingerbread walls and a gingerbread roof, frosting for trim that squeezed on like toothpaste, and candy buttons for door knobs (so we were told). This was not your father's Tinkertoys. None of it snapped together, or made sense.

Like visitors to an alien world, we were quickly out of our element, and Allie—she'd tell me later—begged for acknowledgment of that. *You poor souls! Let us help you build what you cannot possibly know a thing about.* Respect, she'd say. Support. Which I wasn't opposed to; only the asking for it. I thought of other office Christmas parties I had attended over the years, mostly luncheons, how I'd forget the rules, or pout if they had changed. How much to spend on a gift? And for whom? Will anyone like it? Still, as much as I felt like the odd man out at these affairs—and defiant, too—floundering in a sea of indifference, a part of me yearned to be the life of the party; perhaps inside of every Jew is a secret Santa. It's a fragile thing being an outlier and yet, at the same time, wanting to emerge from corners and cloakrooms to be as welcomed into the fold as Saint Nick himself. But just where, outside the womb, does one fit perfectly? I have felt like an outcast among my own tribe, too.

Houses now started to sprout around us, and I envied the expertise. I had assumed our neighbors assembled gingerbread houses every Christmas, and only later learned that, unlike the two of us, they had read and followed instructions. They'd brought paper bags, too, from home, full of gumdrops and glitter, sanding sugar and icing, food coloring, cinnamon sticks, Red Hots. Candy windows, ready-made, with chocolate mullions, and richly colored sills of M&M's. Wax shutters. Dark sprinkles, to look like blackbirds scattered on gingerbread roofs. Ceramic Santas and reindeer in the front yard. Sleigh bells. Chocolate bars they'd chunk into logs, like firewood.

Clearly—with our one small collection of Hanukkah chocolates—we had brought knives to a gunfight; there would be no divine intervention. We cautiously attached our candies, sold in thin gold foil to resemble coins, to our gingerbread roof. They looked like crop circles.

Nevertheless, Luke encouraged us. He wore a crazy sports jacket with flashing lights, like a Christmas tree. Making his rounds table to table, he surveyed our work as I watched the reflection from his coat blinking on Allie's moist forehead like a traffic light. Stop, it seemed to be telling me. *Stop what you are doing right now! Fool.*

Other guests wore vintage sweaters decorated with Santas, elves, reindeer, pine trees. Everyone but us had on something green, or red, including Raquel, my cat whisperer, and advisor on all things that mattered to me: my daughter, Allie, my one office plant and current house renovations. She asked about my cat, Snowflower. I started to tell her that she died some weeks ago, but in trying to say this something died in me a second time and the words never got out. It surprised me, not the loss of words, but the question that seemed to rise simultaneously with my tears: When does it stop? This burden, this grieving. This gift.

Allie touched my hand, and told Raquel about the seizures. I thought of how Snowflower leapt on my bed at night, startling Allie, then scratched at the door when I shut her out and how I had to put her down when she got sick and now I want to crawl into our unfinished house and again cry my head off in this new place we're trying to build with chocolate on the roof, and hope for good things to come. I want to drill or maybe punch a hole in the siding, an opening for her, and pull soft gingerbread sheets over the three of us and just hide.

Raquel didn't know about Snowflower, and is shaken. Her husband, a retired pipefitter, says their three cats are like children, they watch cartoons on TV when Raquel is away or at work, and wait for her at the door upon her return.

Another guest observes that our house is "wanting," as he put it, and suggests it needs more flair. He hands me an extra tube of frosting. It covers a lot of sins, this goo-like glue that holds all the pieces of a dwelling—windows, doors, hearth, chimney—together. I squeeze on a thick bead across the length of the roof, like a multicolored ridge vent. I step back to admire our creation, this building of what our hearts fancied, and pretend we belong here, Luke's party, a star in the tree and a ham in the fridge.

We try to make the most of it. Try to find and build something where we both fit, if not fit in. But under the weight of too much confection, too much arrogance, too much left unsaid, the roof caves in on us, its single story—*our story*, of love and hope, like so many—not yet adequate to support the structure we dreamed. I want to find something more to hold it, hold us, together. A substance that will adhere to our bones, and repel our worst parts. Something magical to shake from a can, like pixie dust, or gypsum, that will secure our future, weave affection and understanding into the fabric of our being, into the walls themselves, put cats and dogs in the yard, deer, too, and a white picket fence around it. Bread in the oven, a log on the fire. Allie's forgiving arms to come home to.

I look around to see if others notice our achievement, this house of cards with its golden roof. I behold upright, proud and charming cottages amidst alpine villages, or wooded glens, sweet homes that beckon you inside to find satisfaction in tight places, cozy up to the hearth and live happily ever after with their soundness, candied symmetry, perfectly gabled roofs and neat woodpiles at the side of gingerbread entrance ways. Hansel and Gretel themselves wouldn't have been able to fill their guts with such finery.

"There are different ways to put a house up," I tell Allie, apologetically.

"And bring them down," she answers, smiling.

The houses are carefully moved to a long table where they stand (or slump), side-by-side, and the winner is chosen. Allie and I are grateful there is no award for last place, which we surely would have taken. We thank our hosts, say goodbyes, and once outside, away from Luke's house, look for tracks in the dark and snowy woods. I turn inward to this other storm: my thoughts, unruly, scattered as if windblown. They land on the instructions I never read. The house that collapsed, improbably, under more sweetness than its walls could bear. My cat. Holidays, family. Stories not written. Guests I wished both to know better—and run from. Running. Always running away. All the waters in the bay cannot extinguish this burning to be alone. To find myself? Does one *find themselves* amidst others? I don't know that world. And yet, and yet...what distance is ever enough? I am lost in this blizzard of thought. Searching, searching. For a lifeboat. The hand of God. I need air, I think, yet it's all around me. I see my breath, it makes its own cloud in the stillness of these woods in this imponderably beautiful December night. I love so inadequately.

I turn in the only direction that makes sense to me, to where Allie is still at my side.

"You're quiet," Allie says.

"Thinking," I tell her. I want to let go, be more open. How is it that what I'm reaching for is also what I'm hiding from? As rich and tumbling a thought as the winter clouds that press down overhead.

The sky would fall again on us that night, but in a good way. The earth moved, too.

Acknowledgments

Many of these stories appeared in slightly different forms in the following journals or publications: *Whisky Blot*; The Preservation Foundation, Inc. *Fan, A Baseball Magazine*; *Beyond Words*; *Flash Fiction Magazine*; *Brilliant Flash Fiction*; *Thoughtful Dog*; *Hypertext Magazine*; Michigan Writers Cooperative Press; Mission Point Press; *Dunes Review*; *JewishFiction.net*; *Made of Rust and Glass*; *Dreamers Creative Writing Magazine*; *Pithead Chapel*; *On the Run*; *Fiction Southeast*; *Jewish Literary Journal*; and *The Great Lakes Review*. I would like to thank the editors of these publications for their belief in my work.

I am especially indebted to the following editors whose vision and clarity moved this collection along: Katey Schultz, for her ongoing support, selfless compassion and wisdom; John Mauk, for his early guidance at the Michigan Writers Cooperative Press; Tanya Muzumdar, for her critical help shaping the manuscript; and Adam Prince, for his input and steadfast encouragement. I also wish to thank my partner and conscience, Anne Arbetter Fischell, for her love, tolerance and invaluable editorial skills, as well.

The following impacted this project one way or another, and for that too I am grateful. So thanks to Ellen Jensen, for her fine and generous ear; Debra Carson; Mark Makie; Erin Alyssa Makie; Wendy and Lenny Newman; Charlie and Nicole Longdon; Amy Gumbleton; Sue Stevens; Doug and Anne Stanton; Rick and Heather Shumaker; Marvin and Lynda Bishop; Dave Murphy; Lewis and Janet Roubal; Ron Braun; Connie Burwell; Susan Makie; Rosemary and Rick Rodriguez; Janine Moniot; Scott Neumann; Patricia Ann McNair; Anne-Marie Oomen; Mary Salisbury; Mary Terzino; Christina Campbell; Gail Bozzano; Jeanne Sirotkin; Benjamin Torres; Club 36, the Oakwood Bistro and Trattoria Stella.

B.L. Makiefsky was born and raised in Detroit, and spent his truly formative years living an itinerant life picking cherries in the Hood River Valley, harvesting hemp in Iowa, working construction in California, writing for a newspaper in West Michigan, crisscrossing the country on motorcycles, hopping trains, and hitchhiking. At Michigan State University, he studied under the writers Albert Drake and Douglas Lawder. Makiefsky was the winner of the 2012 Michigan Writers Cooperative Press chapbook contest for the short story collection, *Fathers and Sons*. His fiction and articles have appeared in numerous literary magazines, and other publications. Currently he is managing editor for the Michigan Writers Cooperative Press.